DOWN IN THE
BARRAQUE

GRANT CARRINGTON

Brief Candle Press Titles
by
Grant Carrington:

Annapolis to Andromeda

Time's Fool and Other Stories

DOWN IN THE BARRAQUE

Brief Candle
Press

Cover design: Brief Candle Press

First Brief Candle Press edition published 2016
www.briefcandlepress.com

ISBN: 978-1-942319-20-7

This book is dedicated to Pat LoBrutto
who suggested I write a book about the barraque
with thanks to
Tom Monteleone, who gave me the idea for the story
and to
Deb Houdek, Michael Bracken, and Lars Hedbor
who helped make it a better book

Kip Marten should have seen it coming but, as usual, he didn't. He was standing on the stage strumming his autar as Flyte Error danced behind his array of electronic instruments and Red Green screamed lyrics into the crowd. Suddenly Green wasn't screaming lyrics but shouting insults back at some spiffie heckler and then he was down in the crowd and Flyte had sped past Kip and was into the crowd with Red. Before Kip had time to put his autar in a safe place, the stage was filled with spiffies and 'quistes, and he had to use his autar to block a fist thrown in his direction. His attacker swore as his fist was cut on the strings and blood stained the instrument's plastic body. Using the neck of the autar as a spear, Kip retreated to the back of the stage, behind the fortress of Flyte's keyboards and drums. But already the customers of the Money Marriage were in the process of tearing it apart.

What the hell, Kip thought. This was all getting to be repetitious. The knowledge that they were going to be involved in another fight didn't make him feel any better. He put down his autar and waded into the mob, sliding easily through with his lanky frame. It wasn't difficult to locate Red Green: he was in the middle of the thickest pile of bodies, roaring his defiance to everybody, spiffy and 'quiste alike. But Flyte Error had disappeared. There was a roar of noise as someone began dismantling Flyte's instruments and the manager of the Money Marriage came out from the back room wielding a club. Kip wiggled his way into the mass of bodies surrounding Red Green, getting bruised and battered by half-deflected blows as he did so. He felt someone's fingers crack under his feet. "Red!" he shouted.

"Hoy! Wade in, Kip. Wade in."

"The squids are here. Let's drift."

"Just a mike, Kip." Green picked up a bruiser who was nearly as big as Green himself and flung him into a mass of attackers. He then began wading out of the melee, shoving a hammy palm in the face of one man while stuffing his fist into the belly of another. He stopped to admire the work of a young woman who was beating up on a spiffy.

"Good work, tufty," he said.

She looked back at him. "Like your music."

"Thanks."

The manager grabbed Kip by the shoulder and spun him around. "You! You're responsible for this!"

"Lay off, mister," Green warned.

The manager wagged a finger in Green's face. "I'm gonna have your asses in The Tower. You'll never get another job in The Zone. I'll see to that."

"Oh, Momma, I'm scared." Green's whine was exaggerated.

The manager's face grew tight and he began to swing the club. Kip tried to grab it and hold the blow back but he was flung away by the force of the manager's swing, the tips of his fingers burning where they had grabbed onto the club. When he got up, Kip saw the manager flying into a group of fighters and Green, grinning, had control of the club. Flyte Error was at his side.

"Let's glide," Flyte said.

"Our instruments . . ." Kip gestured feebly toward the bandstand.

"I'll get new ones. Come on, Kip. Before the squids get here."

The 'quistes had gained control over the spiffies and formed a kind of honor guard or flying wedge with the musicians in the middle. Kip took a breath of fresh air as soon as they reached the outside; he could smell the river. Metal shutters slammed shut as the few businesses still open heard the mob. Someone popped a couple of lights. The girl who had been working over the spiffy handed Kip his autar; other 'quistes carried pieces of Flyte's bank of instruments. Somehow he would put it back together again—Flyte could make puters dance. What he didn't know about them wasn't worth knowing, while Kip and Red just used them for the thousand and one little chores and tasks that everyone else used them for.

The 'quistes poured over the ancient barricades out of The Zone and down the long man-made cliff to the barraque, most of them streaming down the series of narrow switchback stairs while a few agile souls spidered their way down the stonework. The night was alive with shouts and cries and laughter. They were engulfed by the darkness of the barraque and slowly disappeared into the night, slapping the three musicians with the camaraderie of those who had successfully waged a major battle of a war.

The adrenalin still streamed through Kip's veins. The night was still young . . . or at least middle-aged. He wondered what had happened to the battling young tuft. Normally he would have avoided a woman so combative but right now he felt up to handling anything. He had survived the fight with only bruises and a few minor cuts—he would be sore and stiff tomorrow but, hell, that was tomorrow. Now was now and it cried out for more.

They were nearly in Westmeat when Green suddenly veered sharply to the right and pushed open a door. The dim light inside was as bright as daylight to Kip's dark-accustomed eyes. It was hot and stifling inside; the still air seemed to be filled with dust. Kip couldn't remember being here before but there wasn't a joint in the barraque that Red hadn't been in.

"You're not going to get twisted tonight, are you?" Flyte asked.

"We haven't been twisted in weeks," Red said. "Getting drunk's okay but sometimes a guy needs something more. You can drift if you want."

Flyte said nothing but he didn't leave.

The owner held out his puter and the three musicians all thumbed it. It didn't make a peep and the man left them alone with three containers.

"What happened?" Kip asked. "I thought we didn't have the price of a jar." He inserted the nipple at the end of the container's tubing into a socket in his arm and adjusted the flow.

"While you and I were pumping the spiffies, Flyte slipped into the manager's office and chromed the puter. Why do you think I started things?" Green's face was puffy and swollen, one eye nearly shut. His clothes were torn and there was dried blood on his knuckles but he grinned through cracked lips.

"It was crack city," Flyte said. "I passed the word to Red and the rest is ours."

Kip leaned back in the chair. He was feeling good and obviously so was Red. It was harder to tell about Flyte but he had a smirking little grin on his face. Yeah.

The room began to slip away and he was back on the stage again but this time in front of a crowd of thousands instead of a few measly dozens, all crying out his name, adoring and desirous, incredibly lovely women with bedroom eyes, and the music was something else: they were all working smoothly as a team, anticipating chord and time changes fluidly, not the herky-jerky signals to each other that were frequently misread. The lovely women kept changing into the 'quiste tuft who had been working over the spiffy.

Lady Madonna rolled over in her sleep then came suddenly and completely awake. She lay quiet for a long moment, waiting to find out what had roused her. Then she heard a scuffling noise followed by the nearly silent opening of the door to Bird's room followed the barely audible sound of clothes being carefully dropped on the floor.

Only when she was certain that Bird had indeed gone to sleep did The Lady reach out and find an earbud. Then, in utter darkness, she punched out the restricted code for access to the computer's police files of the night's activities. After listening for several minutes, she had the information she needed. She felt a tightness in her chest and lay there a long while, relaxing it away and thinking about Bird. Sooner or later, she was going to have to pay for her activities unless Lady Madonna could convince her to stay away from The Zone.

Even though everything was going strictly according to plan so far, Casey George was worried. There were so many things that could go wrong, so many bits and pieces of information—a major piece could be wrong. But there was no turning back now: that choice had been made when they had abducted the scavenger truck.

"Slow down," Demon Pawn said. "We'll get there too soon. We want to get there just after the first guard leaves to see his tuft."

"Right." Casey slowed down even though every nerve in his body screamed to have this over and done with. The steering wheel felt strange through the skins that covered his body.

When they finally reached the lab, Demon Pawn got into the waste container and Casey and Marsh wheeled it out of the truck into the lab. As they had been promised, only one guard was on duty.

He waved them through and Casey released the breath he hadn't realized he had been holding. They turned the corner and were hidden from the guard but not from the ever-present cameras. They stopped the container in front of an electronics closet and stopped to wipe their brows. Meanwhile Demon Pawn crawled out of the side panel of the container into the closet and closed its door behind him.

Casey and Marsh continued on until they reached the

director's laboratory. Casey pressed a button on the minicorder he held in his palm. "Open," it said.

"ID, please?" the lock asked.

Casey pressed the lock with his thumb and forefinger. It seemed minutes before the lock finally released and the door opened slightly. Casey let go of another breath: the skins had worked. They should—they had cost enough.

They entered the lab, having no way of knowing if Demon Pawn had successfully put the cameras into a loop. "Put anything that looks interesting in the bin," Casey said to Marsh.

With the help of the skins, the minicorder, and the password he'd been given, he quickly was into the guts of the director's computer. So far, all the information they'd been given was correct. He inserted the worm drive. It was knowledge they were interested in, not hardware. It seemed to take hours but the computer's contents were quickly downloaded and his timer had not yet beeped when it was done. Marsh was standing there, looking fearfully at the camera.

"I had to leave space for Pawn," he said when Casey looked at him.

"Let's cover our tracks and go pick him up."

They took two other bags from the container, ripped them open and spread their contents all over the lab. Marsh laughed at the sight.

Casey checked his timer. "Let's go."

As they pushed the container out the door, a cleaning machine turned the corner and came up behind them, spreading disinfectant on the floor and lower walls and wiping everything up, leaving the walls and floor clean and spotless behind it.

"Perfect," Casey said.

They picked up Pawn, passed the guard, and returned to their stolen vehicle. As they drove away, the other guard was returning to his post.

"What do we do now?" Marsh asked.

"Did you copy everything?" Pawn asked.

"Everything," Casey replied.

"Then let's dump the rest of this stuff at Kandalis Reclaimers. Their scavenger will be picking it up in a couple of hours and it'll be melted to slag before they have time to trace it. With any luck at all, they'll never know why we really broke into the lab."

When they reached Kandalis Reclaimers, a man came out of the shadows and, while Casey and Marshall dumped the hardware into the trash container, Pawn walked over to give him the worm drive. Then the man drifted back into the shadows from which he had come. As they drove away, a great sadness came over Casey, as he realized that what was probably the greatest adventure of his life was coming to an end.

Kip came down too soon but Flyte was already waiting for him while Red was still adrift in his own world, undoubtedly screwing dozens of clean spiffy women with perfect teeth and eyes, firm breasts with erect nipples, while he himself was forever hard. Green's dreams were always the same . . . at least according to Green.

"Let's skip," Flyte said.

"And leave Red?" Red's eye was now swollen shut although the rest of his face seemed less puffy.

"He can take care of himself."

Kip pulled the nipple out of his arm. The effort made his bruised muscles scream. As he got up, his stiffened body protested and he had to hold on to the table for support.

Flyte grinned. "It'll be better after you move around a bit."

"Sure," Kip said. "Just let me crawl to the door."

By the time they had reached the door, however, Kip's muscles had quieted down to a mutter, although they promised to make him pay for it later.

Red Green woke up. "Where the hell are you guys going?"

Flyte grinned and kept moving.

Green caught up with them as they were entering an alley. "Leaving without me? I ought to . . . "

"I knew you could take care of yourself," Flyte said.

"Straight on. Where you going?"

"Kandalis Reclaimers. They throw out their scrap tonight and I want to get there before the scavengers pick it up."

Flyte easily scaled fences and other obstacles that Kip and Green crawled over painfully, Red cursing and Kip dragging his autar behind.

"You guys can skip if you want," Flyte said but Red stayed with him and Kip wasn't going to be the first to leave, although his thoughts kept returning to that 'quiste tuft who'd been lumping the spiffy. Well, he wouldn't know where to find her anyway.

Soon they were engulfed in noise. The roar of machinery echoed around them, bouncing off the skyway overhead and augmented by the trucks that jolted down the street. Men stripped to the waist, their bodies glistening with sweat, transferred goods from waiting trucks to the buildings or vice versa. At most of them, a man in a neat jumpsuit watched and made occasional entries in his puter.

They circled round one building and went down another alley, where wary cats watched them but only slowly and reluctantly moved out of their way, to sit in doorways, on trashcans, and on crumbled brick walls until they passed. Green picked up a piece of brick and threw it at one, barely missing it.

"What'd you do that for?" Kip asked.

"Felt like it."

Flyte, several meters ahead of them, was nearly run down by a truck coming out of the alley behind the Kandalis Reclaimers. "Looks like you're too late," Kip said.

"What do you mean?"

"Wasn't that a scavenger truck?"

"Wrong company." Flyte stopped and looked at the already-distant truck. "What the hell were they doing down here?"

Kip and Green helped Flyte into the reclaimers' refuse bin. Almost immediately he cried out and appeared with a complicated electronic rig in his hands. "I don't understand," he said. "Why would they throw something like this out? It's always just bits and pieces."

"What is it?" Green asked.

"Dunno. I'll figure it out when we get home." He handed it to Kip then dived back into the bin. He was there nearly ten minutes before he resurfaced, his clothes packed with faulty electronic parts. "Let's drift," he said.

"Poley." He heard his name from a distance, echoing over and over again, driving away the red pain of his lost hands and he fought up through the fog, like swimming through molasses. "Poley." He broke through the viscous atmosphere and surfaced in his bedroom, groggy and still half-asleep. "Poley."

Most other people would have answered the call by merely acknowledging it but Poley wasn't other people. He rolled off the bedpad and crawled over to his clothes, still feeling as if he were supporting himself on bloody stumps where hands had once been. He took out his controller and toggled the switch with what still felt like insubstantial and unreal hands.

"I'm here."

There was a pause then Benj Walston's voice replaced that of his computer. "What took you so long, Poley?"

"Mister Secretary, I have been up all night. I got to bed just a couple of hours ago."

"You should keep better hours."

"I will be glad to do so, Mister Secretary, if you have no use for the information I gather during those hours." Poley replaced the controller and began crawling toward the table where the dog that had bit him was waiting.

"I need your help."

No shit. Tell me something I don't know, you pompous

twit.

"There was a break-in at the starship laboratory a couple of hours ago."

Poley used the tabletop to pull himself to his feet. "What time is it?"

"Approximately three hours ago. It is now five-thirty."

That jolted Poley. If Walston was up at five-thirty, it had to be serious. He poured himself a drink.

"I need you to keep an eye out in case any of this material shows up in the barraque."

You know damn well it will.

"I have had a list of the stolen items sent to your computer. Get to work on this immediately. This morning."

"Right." *Whatever Walston wants, Walston gets.*

"And, Poley, keep this quiet. Tell no one what has happened."

"My lips are sealed." Poley was certain that half of the people in the barraque already knew.

As soon as Poley knew that Walston was no longer there, he drained the cup and went back to bed.

The coffee had been spooned into the cups and Lady Madonna was waiting for the water to boil. There was nothing special about her morning coffee, unlike the elaborate ceremony she would perform several times during the day for her customers. *Show business. It was all show business.* She heard Bluebird singing in the convenience. Grudgingly she raised her heavy, ancient body and walked over to the convenience and rapped sharply on the door. (Could she really have been so light, just a wisp of a creature, only a few short years ago? No. Those years weren't short.)

"Bird!" she said in a sharp voice. "You should not sing so early in the day."

"But, Lady, I feel so good!"

"That does not matter. Your voice is your most precious possession. You should not sing until you have done your exercises and your voice is warm."

"Yes, Lady."

"And you were up all night. Don't think I don't know. You will destroy your voice with this kind of behavior."

"Yes, Lady."

The kettle began to whistle. "Now hurry up. Before your coffee gets cold."

Lady Madonna trudged wearily back to the table, wondering what Bluebird thought of her. She must look like a toad to the girl, yet there was a time when she had charmed all the young men in the barraque. Well, never mind. She had a greater power now than her attraction had given her when she was young. Bluebird would learn this too, eventually. By the time she had poured the hot water, the young girl joined her, a painful yet pleasant reminder of what The Lady had once been: so slender, moving with a natural, unfeigned, and unpracticed grace, her voice so full and powerful. There were still those in the barraque who remembered The Lady when she had been full of life and youthful hormones. Everybody in the barraque knew The Lady. The men respected her and tipped their hats (if they had any) to her on the street and the women talked about her in hushed tones behind her back.

Once the barraque had been the show place of the city, but that had been many years earlier—when The Lady herself had been a child, it had already begun its long downslide. The Lady remembered the glittering night halls and the way people jammed in from all over the city to see the svana parades that now were a pitiful attempt to regain part of the old barraque's glitter and sophistication.

When she had talked to Bluebird about it, the girl had said, "We'll get it all back some day and we won't have to settle for anything less than the best."

The Lady had smiled. "Yes, some day will come," she had agreed."But we won't be here to see it. Or, if we are, they'll move us to some other place, a new barraque. The city needs us just the way we are."

Bluebird still didn't understand The Lady, even after having lived with her for several years, ever since The Lady had heard her singing on a barraque streetcorner. Of course she hadn't been Bluebird when The Lady had taken her under her wing. It had been The Lady's idea to change her name. "Change your name, child, into what you want to be. That will be the first step and the rest will follow." And she had been right about that too . . . sort of. Everything hadn't followed. Not yet. But it would. It was already happening. It didn't happen all at once, as The Lady herself knew, for her name hadn't always been Lady Madonna.

"Good morning, Lady," Bluebird said.

"Good morning, child. Drink your coffee." Obediently Bluebird sat and sipped briefly at the still scalding liquid while The Lady went to the stove and took out their baked eggs and bread. When Bluebird had first come to her, she had been puzzled and questioned The Lady why she went to all that trouble merely to eat. She no longer questioned, of course; it was accepted that this was the way The Lady chose to live, and now she was beginning to ask The Lady to teach her too the ancient knowledge.

"Where were you last night?" she asked. The girl hesitated. "Don't lie to me."

"I just went to the Money Marriage."

"There was a fight there last night." The Lady was pleased to see the surprised expression on Bluebird's face and just as pleased to see her quickly gain control. "Your voice is a holy gift, child. You put it in danger when you put yourself in danger as well."

"But I enjoy it!"

"Of course you do."

"So what's wrong with it? There are plenty of times you've told me I should have fun and enjoy myself while I'm still young."

The Lady sighed. "And I have also told you to look to the future as well, to prepare for the time when you are as I am now."

"But how can I do both at once? If I'm having fun, I'm not looking to the future. And if I'm looking to the future, I'm not having fun."

"You must learn moderation, child."

"Tonight I'll have fun. Tomorrow I'll look to the future."

"Child . . . "

"After all, when you were my age, you did the same things."

"Which is why I try to prevent you from making the same mistakes I made. If you must make mistakes, child, make new ones."

"With that man, what was his name?"

"Tor Rosedahl. Ah, now there was a man! No skinny whelp like your young barraquistes today. He could lift an entire svana parade float by himself without help from another man. . . "

While The Lady retold still once again the story of the man she had loved so long ago, Bluebird cleaned their breakfast away without any prompting. By the time the tale was finished, Lady Madonna had forgotten their argument and began preparing for the day's clients.

The cool morning air had long ago faded to wherever it hid during the day and the streets were sultry from the unseen sun high above, blocked out by the buildings of the barraque and by those of the city high above the barraque itself. The buildings were old, with the stains of water and sun and birds streaming down their sides, windows covered with rusted sheet metal and splinter-filled wood, occasional windows empty and vacant. The street was pitted and holed; the trucks that carried raw materials into the barraque and carried the work of the barraquistes back out drove slowly and jolted back and forth, rocking from side to side as they negotiated the ruined avenues.

Kip Marten yawned and stretched. Then he winced. He rocked back and forth for a few moments, his head in his hands, trying to find a way to quell the roaring ache inside. After it had subsided a bit, he looked around. Yellow light streamed through large windows, making his head throb. There was a wash basin against one wall. He splashed some water on his face; it was warm and rust-colored but it helped clear his head a little.

He looked around again. He was alone. That ticked him off. They had left him here alone to sleep it off. Then he grinned at the thought of how *they* must be feeling. The grin didn't hurt too badly this time. Slowly, he began remembering the previous night's events. It had been a real drag-outer. And there was the girl. He couldn't get the girl out of his mind. And Flyte Error's ecstasy over his haul from Kandalis Reclaimers.

"Are you going to vedge on your ass all day?" Kip jumped as Red Green's voice reverberated off the hard walls of the empty room. He looked up to see Green filling up one of the doorways. He didn't seem to be suffering from the previous night. Kip should've known.

"Where the hell have you been?" Kip growled.

"Out rustling up some food while you were getting your beauty sleep. God knows you need it." Green threw his pack down on the floor.

Kip walked over to where Green had flung himself to the floor. "Where's Flyte?" Green reached into the pack and handed Kip a piece of crumbly bread. "What the hell is this?"

Green took out a flask and poured some wine into a bowl. "Day olds." He dipped the bread into the wine.

Marten followed suit after scraping off some of the larger mold spots. "More like three days," he said, spraying crumbs all over the floor.

Green shrugged. "Whatever."

"So where the hell's Flyte?"

"Dead."

Kip dropped his bread. "What?"

Green was unperturbed. "Dead to the world. Snoring like a baby."

"You son of a bitch!" He reached into Green's sack. "What else have you got?" He pulled out a piece of meat. "Where did you get this?"

"That's mine!" Green grabbed the meat out of Kip's hand and jammed it back into his sack, which he pulled possessively to his side.

"Where did you tag that?" Kip repeated.

"None of your damn business," Green growled.

"Are you two still at it?" Flyte Error stood in the doorway.

"Risen from the dead?" Green got down on his knees and began salaaming Flyte Error.

"You eaten yet?" Kip dipped some more crumbly bread into Green's wine.

"No. And I ain't gonna eat none of that swill. I'll wait and get something decent." He squatted next to Kip and looked at him for a long moment before finally saying, "What do you know about brains?"

"I know he ain't got any." Kip made a toss of his head in Green's direction.

"Yeah." Flyte Error sat down on the hard cement floor and hugged his knees. "What about telepathy?"

"You mean mind reading?"

"Sort of. You believe in it?"

Kip thought a moment. Flyte Error's seriousness was unnerving. "Nah. If it really existed, we'd have been doing it long ago. It's just fantasy, that's all."

"Maybe. Maybe not. Puters do it, you know."

"Puters don't think," Green snarled.

"Maybe. Maybe not. But they can dump the contents of their cores into the cores of other puters. If we knew how to do that . . . "

"We'd be puters. No thanks." Green tore off another chunk of moldy bread.

"But just think of the possibilities, the knowledge." Flyte Error was staring off into space. "We'd know what each other was thinking and feeling."

"I don't want your dirty fingers in my brain." Green pulled the bread out of the wine dripping wet and spattered wine all over the front of his shirt as he dropped it into his open mouth. A soggy chunk of bread broke loose and landed on his trousers. "Shit. Everybody'll think I pissed in my pants."

"Kip?"

"What?"

"What do you think? It'd make us one tight little band, don't you think?"

"Yeah. We'd probably play better if we knew what Red was going to do at any time. But I'm not sure I'd want to know. Anyway, we'd be a lot better if we rehearsed more often."

"We already rehearse enough," Red said. "Hell, we rehearse too much."

Flyte Error sighed. "If only we were puters."

"Keep at it," Red said. "You're almost there."

They separated, each in search of something different—Green to check out the bars and brothels, Flyte Error to scavenge the bins of the factories and warehouses, Kip in a vague search for the young woman at the performance in The Zone the previous night.

It was nearly afternoon by the time Poley stepped out onto the streets of the barraque.

"Nothing, Poley," the man said. "I haven't seen anything electronic in weeks."

"You're sure?" Poley peered at him, trying somehow to look past his eyes and into his mind. Sometimes it worked but this man was unmoved by Poley's stare. "Well, if anything comes up, let me know immediately. I'll make it well worth your while."

The man smiled, revealing two gold teeth. "Walston, huh? If he wants it, it'll cost him dear." He did a good imitation of Poley's stare. "If you'd let me know what I'm looking for, it would be a big help."

Poley grimaced. "If I knew, I'd tell you. But Walston won't give me any more information."

"Of course he won't." It didn't sound as if the man believed Poley but it didn't really matter. "Have you tried Sky Balboa?"

"Already been there. He doesn't know any more than you do."

"Well, there you are then."

Poley walked out of the pawnshop, not really surprised. He walked slowly, nodding to those who knew him. Anyone smart enough to break into the starship lab wouldn't be putting this stuff out on the street. There had always been rumors about an underground resistance of some kind but Poley had never taken them seriously—whenever people were disgruntled, which was most of the time, they'd talk about overthrowing the upper city but nobody was ever going to do anything about it. Just talking about it made them feel better. There was no such movement; if there was, he would have found out about it. You don't keep things like that hidden for very long. Which meant that whoever had broken into the starship lab didn't come from the barraque and Walston had sent him on a wild goose chase.

The sweet smell of warm dough engulfed Kip as he walked past one of the bakeries. Outside, a couple of workers were talking in a language Kip didn't understand. Down the street, at the mouth of an alley, an old man and an old woman embraced, the woman talking continually until Kip was out of earshot. A young woman hobbled across the street and Kip had to look twice to be sure: she had only one leg. It looked so strange to him, just one well-shaped leg coming out from under her dress.

The eerie music of a violin fell from the second floor of

a building where a woman was barking out instructions. Kip stopped to listen to it, trying to imprint it in his mind so he could later reproduce it on the autar. This wasn't the first time he had tried to do something like this but, no matter how hard he concentrated, by the time he got back to the warehouse, the music would be gone from his mind.

He rushed to catch up to a woman who looked like the young woman of the previous night but, when he caught up to her, she looked nothing like the object of his search.

This was ridiculous. He didn't know her name, he didn't know where she lived—he had as much chance of finding her as Flyte Error had of reading Red Green's mind. He should've gone with Red. It was too early for the gang to be gathering— like Red, Flyte, and Kip, they would be just getting up and going out to find some food before they drifted in to The Oyster for a night of music and fun.

The hell with it. He'd go back and see what Flyte was up to. Maybe they could have a decent conversation without Red there.

On the other side of the street, a small man came out of a store, looked around, then went into the bar next door. Kip recognized him—Robert Poley was one of Benj Walston's spies. He came out of the bar and went into the next one, obviously looking for something. Or someone. Kip didn't like it. It meant trouble for someone. He thought of going across and trying to find out what or who Poley was looking for then thought better of it. It could only get him in trouble with Poley and that was the kind of trouble Kip didn't need.

As Poley had expected, Skarys was at his favorite joint. He took a seat next to the bouncer. "Working tonight?" he asked.

Skarys looked at him for a long moment, long enough for the tender to slide a bottle in front of Poley.

"Maybe. Who wants to know?"

"Who cares? Just making conversation." Poley uncapped his bottle and took a long drink from it.

"Sure." Skarys watched Poley wipe his mouth with the back of his hand. "And I'm going to be chief marshal in this year's svana parade."

"Wouldn't surprise me at all."

"I might work tonight. I might not. So what?"

"You heard what happened at the Money Marriage last night?"

"Yeah. There was a little bit of a tiff. Happens every night."

"People got hurt."

"People get hurt every day." Skarys rubbed his scarred knuckles. "Sometimes I'm the one who has to do the hurting."

"Other than that, though, it was a quiet night."

"If you say so."

"You didn't hear of anything else happening last night, did you?"

"Did you?"

"Too quiet, don't you think?"

Skarys leaned back and took a long drink before finally answering. "I don't get paid to think."

"It's got Walston scared."

"Walston is always scared."

"He wants to know what's going on."

"Uh-huh. What's in it for me?"

"What do you need?"

"What does anybody need? More credit." Skarys drained his bottle and signaled to the tender.

"No problem for Walston. He's always done right by you. He'll pay whatever price is necessary. You know that. Knowledge. That's all that's important to him."

"Yeah. I'll see what I can find out. Who was playing there last night?"

"Where?"

"The Money Marriage."

"Red Green and his group."

Skarys laughed, a bark that seemed as if it would tear his throat apart. "There's your answer then. Those guys are trouble-makers just for the hell of it."

"There are other . . . "

"Just like a wild young fellow I used to know ten years ago. A fellow by the name of Poley. He thrived on trouble and he thrived on causing it."

As Skarys talked, Poley's face turned cold and hard, masking whatever feelings might be underneath. He took out his knife and began digging under his fingernails with it. "That Poley is dead," he said. "Dead and gone. He died in the Tower."

Skarys looked at Poley's face then looked away. "A lot of good men have been left in the Tower," he said.

Poley looked at his bottle for a long time then said in a low, almost inaudible voice, "A lot of good men."

Skarys got up. "Well, if you want some information, I guess I'm going to have to find myself some work for the night. But, while you're waiting, why don't you go ask Green yourself?" Skarys flipped his thumb toward a table at the back of the bar, where Green was sprawled, asleep or drunk. "I'll leave you a message where to find me . . . as soon as I know myself."

Before Skarys could reach the door, Poley was already walking slowly toward the table where Red Green was sprawled. Looking back, Skarys grinned as he saw Poley approaching the young musician like some kind of predatory animal stalking prey that was totally unaware of its danger. Poor Green, Skarys thought as he left the bar.

Poley reached the young man's table, slowly pulled out an ancient chair, and sat in it slowly and carefully, like a cobra getting ready to strike. He took a long drink from his bottle then set it down quietly, barely disturbing the dust. He sat there a long time, studying Green, whose head was resting on his forearm while the other arm was stretched out across the table.

Finally Poley said, "Green" in a voice that could not have been heard more than a meter away. Green did not move. Poley reached out and touched Green's stretched-out arm and said his name again. There was still no reaction.

Poley waited a moment longer then reached out with both hands and lifted Green's head from its resting place. "Green!" he said sharply, though only slightly louder than he had spoken before.

The young man's eyes opened and looked at Poley for a brief unfocussed moment then closed again. Poley let go with his right hand and slapped him lightly on the cheek, little more than a brush. Green's eyes snapped open again.

"I want to talk to you, Green." Poley let go of Green's head and it fell back down on his forearm.

"Go away."

"Where were you last night, Green?"

"Lots of places. Go away."

"You were playing at the Money Marriage."

"So what?"

"There was a fight there."

Green raised his head and looked at Poley, a beatific smile on his face. "There sure was."

"What caused it?"

"Beats hell out of me."

"What do you think caused it?"

Green shrugged and immediately winced. He sat back in his chair and ran his fingers through his unruly hair. "The same thing that always causes fights. Some asshole steps on some other asshole's foot and they get pissed at each other. Or maybe it was over some little bit of tuft. You know how it is."

"It happened at the Money Marriage. They have better clientele than that."

Green grinned again. "Topsiders don't fight?"

"Not like you do."

"Hey, we brought a few our own people too, you know? They like us down here and they follow us wherever we go. Ain't no law against that, is there?"

"Not yet. But if you keep causing riots wherever you play,

there might be one."

"Then we'll have to make a new one. Like, no topsiders in barraque bars."

"I'm not a topsider, Green. You know that."

"You might as well be."

"Look, you need credit. Cooperate with me and I'll see that you get it."

Green stood up and grabbed the back of the chair for balance. "I don't need your dirty money, Poley, and I don't want it." He grinned. "But I could use some of this." He picked up Poley's bottle, chugged half of it, then walked out of the bar with the bottle.

Poley stood up angrily but stopped almost immediately and grinned at Green's back as he left. Then he went back up to the bar for another bottle. The day was still young.

When Kip returned to the warehouse, Flyte Error was sitting in the middle of a large and mostly barren room, intently examining the electronic rig, the room's concrete floor scattered with electronic parts–diodes and triodes, cracked transistors, wires of all colors and sizes, transformers, chipped circuit boards. Boxes of electronic parts, all carefully marked, were scattered around. Flyte put a jeweler's loupe in his eye and examined the rig more carefully then softly said "Damn!" He removed the loupe and rubbed his eyes then got up slowly and walked around the room's litter, stretching his cramped legs. He stopped for a moment in front of an empty window frame but he didn't seem to notice the ever-noisy barraque factory district outside or the long rusty barge slowly rotting away on the other side of the river, next to the reclamation plant. His gaze was inward.

He turned around, still lost in thought, then his pale blue eyes focused on Kip, standing inside the doorless doorway, hesitant about interrupting Flyte's ruminations. "How long have you been here?"

"Just got here." Kip finally entered the room. "You found anything useful?"

"I don't know. Here." Flyte picked up the electronic rig he had found in the refuse bin and handed it to Marten.

"What is it?"

"How the hell should I know?"

"What do you think it is?"

Flyte sat down and leaned wearily against the wall. "I don't know and I don't care."

"Then what the hell are you giving it to me for?" Marten shoved the rig back at Flyte, who set it down carefully on the floor.

"It's not what it is that concerns me, Kip, it's what it can be."

"So what the hell can it be?"

Flyte looked pensive a moment. "I'm not sure yet."

"Lord!" Marten started to get up but Flyte pulled him down by the shoulder. He tried to hand one of the plugs to Kip but Marten pulled himself away. "What the hell are you doing with that thing?"

"I want to try something."

"Well, try it on someone else. Like yourself. You don't know what the hell that thing is. It could kill me."

"I already tried it on myself. It isn't going to kill you."

Reluctantly, Kip put the plug into the receptacle at the base of his skull. It was just like going to school all over again, where he had met Flyte Error and Red Green, first as holo-classmates until Red had dropped out and Flyte had tracked both of them down on the streets of barraque. Even then, Flyte knew how to get around the city puters to find out what he wanted to know.

There were several other plugs among the tangle of electronic straps and they were all connected. Flyte chose one for himself—now wires and leads connected them to each other. Finally the small blond-haired man was finished. He looked at Kip and grinned.

"Feel anything?"

"Am I supposed to?"

"Just checking."

Flyte picked up a jack from the tangle of wires in front of him and plugged it into a wall socket before Kip could stop him. There was a sudden buzzing in his ears, like a couple of hundred distant bees. Something intelligible seemed to be hidden in that buzz but he couldn't make it out. A familiar smell that he couldn't quite place arose in the back of his nose and a shimmering transparency danced in front of his eyes, images that he couldn't quite focus on.

"How about now, Kip?" He could hear Flyte clearly through the buzzing.

"What the hell's going on, Flyte?"

"Concentrate."

"On what?" There was no answer. "What the hell do you want me to concentrate on, Flyte?"

"Just a mike, Kip, just a mike. I'm trying to get it but I lose it every time I have to talk to you."

Kip tried to concentrate on the buzzing and the fleeting images in front of his eyes but he couldn't make anything out.

"Concentrate on Children of the Undercity."

"What?"

"Children of the Undercity. You know the show, don't you?"

"Sure. But why the hell would I want to concentrate on that crap?"

"Look, just do as I say, okay?"

"All right, all right." Kip's voice was surly but he really didn't mind as much as he pretended to. He actually enjoyed the show, about Stefan Coldrider, who had saved a topsider from a barraquiste mob. He had his own dreams of doing something similar some day, living in the upper city as an HV star, with perfect and gorgeous upper city women begging for him to make love to them. Except now, when he thought about it, they looked an awful lot like that 'quiste tuft last night . . .

"Hey, he's going to learn to play autar!"

"What?"

"Stefan Coldrider. He's learning to play autar. Aren't you concentrating?"

"What in the Lord's name are you talking about?"

"Concentrate on the show. Concentrate on Stefan Coldrider learning to play autar."

Kip thought about it. Wouldn't that be something? Coldrider learning to play autar! Kip could be just like him. The title of the show seemed to hang in the air in front of Kip in letters of fiery red: CHILDREN OF THE UNDERCITY and a voice intoned, "The ongoing story of young people in the barraque who struggle their way upward to success." It seemed as if the show's hero was sitting in front of him right now, his form materializing from the shimmering images, pushing them away to the fringes of his sight, and Coldrider's autar emerged from the buzzing in his ears. It was awful, but not as awful as Kip had been when he had first picked up the autar. Well, that made sense. This was only an HV show, after all. They had to take a few liberties with reality or nobody would be interested. If only Kip Marten's life had the same plot as that of Stefan Coldrider.

This was better than watching it in The Oyster with dozens of other people standing round making rude comments, putting the show down, with Kip trying to pretend that he didn't really believe that someone like Stefan Coldrider could actually exist. He wondered how many others were like him, hiding their beliefs under a veneer of cynicism and sarcasm.

"Kip?" Flyte Error's voice seemed to come from inside his head.

"What?"

"Don't say it. Just think it."

"Will you shut up? I want to watch this thing."

"I'm recording it. You can watch it later."

"Fuck you."

Coldrider and the music he was trying to make suddenly disappeared. Flyte had yanked the jack out of the wall. Kip felt empty, as if he had lost the most important thing in his life. And it was just a lousy afternoon HV show!

"What the hell did you do that for?"

"You experienced it, didn't you? Children of the Undercity?"

"Yeah, of course I . . . " Kip stopped. "You did that, didn't you? I mean, the . . . the thing there." Kip gestured toward the rig. "Hey, how about that? We've got our own HV now. That's great."

"It's not the same, Kip."

"What do you mean? I saw it. Coldrider was standing right there and . . . "

"It was all in your mind, Kip, not on an HV stage. This is something new. I've never heard of anything like this before."

Kip thought about it for a moment. "In my mind? Yeah, I guess it was, wasn't it? And when you talked to me there, at the end . . . "

"I didn't talk to you. I thought to you."

"That's what you were babbling about this morning, wasn't it?" Kip looked at the tangled electronic straps on the floor in front of them. "What is this thing? It's neat but it's just a little better than an HV setup. So what?"

"I don't know yet. But I've got some ideas. This thing could do us a lot of good, if we don't get caught with it. What really worries me is . . . " Flyte stopped to scratch his head. "Why did Kandalis Reclaimers throw out something like this? It must be worth a fortune. It doesn't make any sense at all."

"We need to get Red in on this."

"I don't know if that's a good idea."

"Why not? We're blood. That's all that matters."

Flyte took a long time before he answered. "Okay. Go get him."

"Oh, no." Kip held up his hands. "You've got to come too. It's got to be both of us."

Once again, Flyte took a while to think about it before he started gathering up things and putting them away.

"Hi, Casey, this is the Old Man."

"Yeah. What's up?" Despite the difference in their ages and the fact that The Old Man Himself had practically raised Casey as if he were his own son, the son the Old Man had never had, they tried to treat each other as if they were the same age and had been friends all the their lives, which was essentially true for Casey.

"Just sitting here, looking out the window, down the alley, thinking and reminiscing."

They talked for a little while longer until The Old Man Himself ended the call and Casey went for a walk that took him to an alley several blocks away from Kandalis Reclaimers, where Demon Pawn was waiting for him.

"Are you sure this is safe?" Casey asked. "I thought you said we shouldn't meet again or acknowledge each other."

"There's been a change. I've been given some information and it has to be disseminated and you're the best one to do it."

"Me? Why do I have to do your dirty work?"

"People need to know and, if it comes from you, they're more likely to listen and believe. Everybody else thinks I'm incompetent and don't know what I'm talking about half the time." Demon Pawn gave a self-satisfied smile. "And they're usually right."

"Where'd you get this so-called information?"

"It came from higher up in the organization so I have to believe it and so do you. We really don't have any other choice."

Casey George looked up the walls of the building. "What about those flying spics of theirs?"

"Walston only sends them out at night. He's afraid we'll find out about them."

"Okay." Casey George gave an exaggerated sigh. "What's this information I have to spread around the barraque?"

The Oyster was nearly empty when Kip and Flyte entered, daylight barely filtering through the dirty windows. The lights were dark and low and most of the customers were in dirty, oily clothes. Old Toothless Johnny, short and slightly bent over, was at the bar, already half-loaded. His face was a mess—a mouth with only a few teeth left in it, a bulbous nose with warts growing in all directions, some with hairs growing out of them. A young couple sat at one of the booths, making Kip more aware of the fact that he had no lady. The tender motioned toward the back room, where they found Green sprawled across a table, his hand still gripping an empty bottle as if his life depended on his maintaining possession of it.

Flyte Error turned Green's hand to look at the label. Green did not react at all. "Lord, where'd he get the credit for this stuff? This is ten leagues beyond what he usually drinks. I hope he didn't drink up all our credit."

"It's a good thing we don't have a gig tonight." Kip sat down in the chair next to Green and stretched out.

"We could've rehearsed. We were pretty sloppy last night, even before the fight broke out. We're never going to get anywhere if we don't get tight."

"You know it. I know it." Kip motioned toward Red. "But this is the only kind of tight he knows."

"We oughta dump him."

"Ah, we can't do that. He's the one everybody comes to see. The spiffies think he's real barraque and the 'quistes all wish they were like him."

"So? There are dozens more like him. We don't have to put up with this kind of crap all the time."

"Sure, there are dozens more like him and they'll all be the same. He's ours, Flyte. We're not going to walk out on him. We're blood. We've always been blood."

Flyte Error started toward the front of the Oyster. "I'm going to see how much credit we've got left. You want your usual?"

"Sure."

Kip lifted Red's head and pried open an eyelid. An unseeing eyeball stared back at him. He let go and lowered the singer's head gently back to the table. It was so quiet he could hear the rats scrambling in the walls. Someone slid into the seat opposite. Kip looked up to see Casey George grinning at him.

Casey looked at the bottle in Red's hand. "Poley's brand," he said.

"Yeah? So?" The knowledge didn't make Kip feel any better so he tried to glower at Casey but it didn't have the effect he wanted. Casey George just continued to grin.

"Poley could have left it here, of course."

"Sure. He could've passed out, like Red, and forgotten all about it when he left."

"On the other hand, I've never known Poley to leave anything without a purpose."

"What are you trying to say?"

"Me? Nothing. I have no idea what this means." Casey George flicked the bottle with his fingernail and it made a dull hollow plastic thump. "Do you have any idea what it means?"

"It means that for once Red got his hands on some good stuff and that we're without credit again. It won't be the first time."

Flyte Error set down a bottle in front of him. "We've still got plenty of credit. Red didn't buy that bottle. At least not with our credit. Someone else must've bought it for him." Flyte motioned toward Casey George without looking at him. "What's he doing here?"

"Just stopped by to say a friendly hello." Casey got up. "And now I'll say a friendly goodbye." He grinned at Kip again. "Goodbye." He walked out to the front bar and started talking to the workers and old-timers there.

"What'd he want?" Flyte asked as soon as Casey was gone.

"He said that's Poley's brand."

"Poison."

"What?"

"Poison. Trouble. That's what he is. I don't like him. I don't like him and I don't like Red Green. They're both nothing but bad news."

"Hey, what happened? Yesterday you and Red was tighter'n he is now. We wouldn't have no credit if you two didn't work like twins. If we made music the way you two made that deal go down last night, we'd be playing spiffies every night."

"Big deal!"

"Yeah! I think it is."

"They'll cut your balls off, Kip. You want to make music, good music, even more than me. He don't care. He just wants to get laid and have everybody look at him like he was some kind of little plastic god."

"What's the matter with you, Flyte?"

Flyte Error leaned forward and looked intently at Kip. "We can make it, you and me, because we care. It's not just some ego trip. He's dead cargo, Kip, he's holding us down."

"He ain't and you know it. He's the one that makes it for us, you know. He's got, what is it? Karma?"

"Charisma?"

"Yeah. We don't have that. We're afraid of making fools of ourselves out there but, Red, he just don't give a damn. You couldn't do what he does and neither could I."

"But he's no musician!"

"So what? He's a performer and that's what you and I ain't. And that's what they want, all of them, spiffies and 'quistes alike. You'n'me, we're just so much wallpaper to them."

"That sucks, Kip."

"But it's true and you know it. And that's why we need him more than he needs us."

"You bet your fuckin' ass," Red said. He looked at Flyte Error and grinned. "How they hangin', Flyte?"

"Where'd you get that damn bottle, Red?" Flyte demanded.

Red lifted his hand and looked at the bottle as if he had never seen it before. "Hey, how about that? Damn good stuff." He lifted it to his mouth to get the last taste he could. "We oughta drink this all the time. We can afford it now, can't we?"

"Where'd you get it? Who bought it for you?"

"Nobody bought it for me. I took it. I always take whatever I want. You know that, Flyte."

"Who'd you take it from, then?"

Red grinned foolishly again. "Poley. And I'll tell you something, Flyte: he ain't nearly as tough as he thinks he is."

Flyte stared at Red with a look of distaste on his face. He turned to Kip. "You stay here and babysit him. I'm going back to the warehouse."

Red stared at his back as Flyte left The Oyster. "Now what the hell's eatin' him? He can play the hell out of those damn keyboards but I don't understand him at all."

Lady Madonna lay down wearily on her ratty couch and massaged her temples. There would be no more customers today. She had seen them all, listened to their tales and gossip, given them herbal teas and other home remedies that had thousand-year pedigrees, sometimes laced with something more modern if the occasion warranted it. Most of them left feeling better, mostly by the simple act of talking about their troubles to someone who was not involved.

The bell over her doorway tinkled, announcing the arrival of someone she wasn't expecting. She got up and pushed aside the tasseled and spangled curtain of her "inner sanctum." And then she stopped, caught completely by surprise.

"Good day, Lady," Casey George said.

"Well. I never thought the day would come when you would want to have your fortune told."

"I don't." The young man sat down jauntily on the easy chair in her outer chamber and she resented the way he seemed to be taking over her abode. But, oh, he looked so young and handsome, reminding her of Tor Rosedahl and the days when all her friends were young and handsome and pretty.

"What do you want then?"

"Tell me *your* fortune, Lady Madonna."

"I have grown old and fat. My fortune is already spent."

Casey George raised his eyebrows. "I never knew you had any fortune at all."

"Youth was my fortune, as it is yours now."

"Ah, yes. They say you were quite attractive in your time."

"Judge for yourself, Casey George."

An image of her younger self appeared between them, slender, her face a little too angular for beauty but with eyes that shone with merriment and mischief, a friendly smile with a hint of mystery. As for her body, it would never have appealed to those who liked too much of any one thing but it was balanced in all its charms in such a way that few men could have resisted. The image pirouetted in front of Casey George, its feminine charms hidden yet occasionally revealed by the shimmering robe it wore, then it faded from view.

Casey George smiled. "It must be very convenient to have an HV stage hidden here. What else do you have hidden, I wonder."

"You didn't come here to talk shop, Casey George, or to listen to me reminisce about my youth."

Casey George got up and peered around the room. "Where is that young girl of yours?"

"Bluebird? She is out, getting into some kind of trouble, I would imagine. That's what young people do, isn't it?"

Casey George peered and her and smiled. The smile nearly broke her heart. It was so like . . .

"Are you implying that I am in some kind of trouble?" Casey asked.

"Are you going to tell me that you're not? It will be the first time in twenty years that you haven't been."

"Ah. What kind of trouble am I in? Tell me, Lady Madonna."

"Your soul is in trouble, Casey George. Your very being is in danger of being cast into the hellfires of perdition."

"Ah, don't try to scare me with that superstitious drivel. I am not one of your old men or old women, sitting in the square, trying to warm themselves with the rays of times long over and done with. Those days are long gone, Lady, and you know it as well as I do."

"The barraque shall rise again."

"Don't mock me, Lady."

"I am not mocking you, Casey George, no more than I mock myself and the men and women I grew up with. But you are wrong to call it superstitious drivel. There is more to my words than you can understand now. But when you become one of those old men . . . perhaps I should say *if* you become one of them . . . then perhaps you will understand."

"It will be a different time then, Lady, and its people will be different."

"Some things are eternal. But I don't have eternity myself and if your only reason for coming is to play these word games with me, then I must ask you to leave."

"No, Lady, I came to ask your help."

"My help? I cannot keep you forever young. If I could do that, then I would not be what I am today."

"You are the one playing word games, not I. I ask your help and you . . . "

"What do you need my help for, Casey George?"

"You care about the barraque and its people, don't you?"

"Of course."

"I wish to help them."

"And yourself."

"The starship is finished."

"You don't know what you're talking about. It is far from being finished. It will be years, maybe decades . . . "

"Perhaps. But *our* work is done." Casey's gaze fixed on

(33)

some distant vision. "I remember what it was like here before they started to build the starship. I was only a little boy then but I knew what it was like to beg for crusts of bread, to be kicked by topsiders who came down slumming to the barraque."

"That was twenty, thirty years ago."

"Then they needed us, our backs, our brawn, to make their stinking chemicals, to forge their tools, to do all the back-breaking work that they were too dainty to do for themselves, risking our lives for them, hollowing out that damn asteroid and preparing it for their little games."

"The starship has been good for the barraque. It has brought us jobs, credit. Is that such a bad thing? I remember the days before the starship better that you, Casey George, and I remember the days before the days. The barraque has prospered under the starship."

"But it's all coming to an end . . . now! Not tomorrow, not ten years from now, but now."

The Lady shook her head. "No. There are still years and years of work to be done on it."

"But it will not be our work. They don't need us any longer. Most of the work that's left is the refining of what has gone on before. The engines are built and installed. All the work that's to be done on them will be done in orbit. The passages and the rooms are all hollowed out. They need only to be made fit for people to live in. And so it goes. The brute work is done. All that's left is the thousand and one finishing details. Years? Yes. It will take them years. But they won't need us to help them any more."

Lady Madonna stared at Casey George. "How do you know all this?"

"I have eyes. And so do you, my lady. You cannot be so blind. The knowledge is there. There have been cutbacks and layoffs."

"A few men. Only a few."

"A few at Kandalis Reclaimers. A few at State Refineries. A few more here, a few more there. Have you counted up how many a few adds up to?"

"No doubt you have."

"There have been over two hundred men laid off in the past three months, another three hundred on partial time . . . "

"They were working overtime."

"Three shifts, around the clock. Now nearly half of our industry is running only two shifts."

"That is still better than only one, or none at all."

"This is just the beginning. They're not so stupid up above. They do it just a little bit at a time. If they did it all at once, there would be riots and they know it."

"So what do you want me to do about it?"

"I have eyes, Lady, and I have ears. But no barraquiste needs either of them to know how much power and influence you wield."

"I am just a . . . "

"We will need your support when the time comes. Meanwhile, just let people know what's happening and what's going to happen. Don't let them all be taken by surprise. You owe them that much."

"I don't owe anyone . . . "

"But you care, Lady, you care. You care about what happens to the barraque and its people. Just do what's right. That's all I ask."

"You ask more than that, Casey George."

"Think of what I have said." He opened the door and stood in the doorway a moment. "You know I'm right."

"Wait!" But he was gone and she really had nothing to say to him after all. She had not felt so helpless in years. He had played her like a musical instrument until she could do nothing but protest. And how could she have been so blind not to have seen the signs? As soon as he had said that starship was finished, she had begun to recognize the omens. But it was not that simple. She had been misled . . . or, at least, vital information had been withheld from her while she had been engrossed in training Bluebird. And meanwhile she had lost priceless time forever.

"Computer! I want the records of hirings and layoffs and cutbacks in the barraque and the upper city for the last six months. . . . And what starship contracts have been finished or begun in the same period." She would double-check on everything that Casey George had told her but she was already certain that he was correct.

Everything else that had been taken out of the laboratory could be replaced, but the navigation web was without price. Designed and constructed by Daul Magwin, one of the brightest and most brilliant scientists of the time, it was irreplacable. But Magwin was also erratic and overbearing: with his reputation, he could do as he pleased, and he usually did. He worked alone, confiding in no one while relying on everyone he could cajole into letting him know their secrets. Most of the work on the control web had been done by Daul Magwin and Daul Magwin alone. It was to have been the crowning achievement of his life, and it had been . . . until it had been stolen. No one but Daul Magwin could recreate it and Magwin had died before turning it over to the laboratory, died while still testing and perfecting it.

As Casey George headed back toward Westmeat, he began to feel better. He hadn't wanted to face Lady Madonna but Pawn had insisted that he talk to her as soon as possible. He thought he had put a good face on it but he wondered if The Lady had been able to see the nervousness and uncertainty that he had tried to keep in check.

It would be a lot easier talking to the workers in the bars of Westmeat, many of whom had worked with him hollowing out the innards of the asteroid. He knew where he would find Dumb Red, his foreman ten years ago who was anything but dumb. It was Red who had taught him how to handle a jackhammer in that airless gravityless nothingness. The scientific brains had designed one for use overhead but it couldn't do its job without having a lot of recoil and the big brains couldn't foresee all the problems. It was Dumb Red who had figured out how to handle one without immediately sending its handler spinning around his safety cords and environment hoses.

Dumb Red would listen to him and he would spread the word.

As he crossed the street, he caught a glimpse of The Lady's girl. Was she following him? It would be just like The Lady to set her after him, but the girl wasn't very good at it. All the tension drained from him. This was going to be fun.

He continued walking as if he wasn't aware of the girl, trying to figure out exactly how he would deal with her. Finally he walked into the Oyster. He could see her waiting in the shadows of a doorway.

After Flyte Error left, Red sprawled asleep again. It was the same old song; as Flyte had said, Red could take of himself, so Kip went back out into the late afternoon, watching the kids at play on the square, past the old men with their bottles and patches, past the old ladies who waved to him, the young women who didn't even bother to notice him, none of them the battling young tuft at the Money Marriage. He wandered around for about half an hour before finally going back to the warehouse.

Flyte Error was lying on the cement floor of the abandoned warehouse, his synthkeys on his lap. What would happen if he tried to rouse Flyte? Was he watching HV the same way they had before or was this something different? He started forward just as his bandmate stirred, punching something on the keyboard. Kip waited a long moment, still indecisive but thinking that Flyte was all right if he could still play with his synthkeys. At last he softly called out his bandmate's name.

For a long moment, nothing happened then Flyte Error hit

one of the buttons on the synthkeys and opened his eyes, his gaze on something in a nonexistent far distance before focusing on Kip. "Where's Red?" he asked.

"At the Oyster. I had to come back and see how you were doing. What were you doing?"

Flyte smiled a wan smile. "You won't believe what I was doing. I'm not sure I believe it myself. I sure as hell don't understand it, that's for sure." He stood up shakily and paced the room.

"So what were you doing, man? Spill."

Flyte kept pacing. "Things are just so damn confusing, Kip. I don't know what I should do."

"Well, let me help you."

Flyte pulled up one of the rickety chairs. "If I tell you, can you keep it from Red?"

Kip thought a moment. "Sure, if it's so damn important to you. But I don't like it."

Flyte looked intensely at Kip. "If Red gets breath of what's going down, it could mean trouble for all of us, big trouble."

"What kind of trouble?"

Flyte was quiet for so long that Kip began to think he wasn't going to answer until he said in a voice so low it was almost a whisper, "The Tower. For all of us."

Kip felt a shiver. "You're kidding." You didn't joke about The Tower. No one did.

Flyte Error shook his head slowly as he said, "This isn't bullshit, Kip. This thing." He gestured to the device that he had raided from Kandalis Reclaimers. "This is like nothing I've ever heard about."

"So what is it?"

"It's something from the starship lab. Someone stole it from there."

"How do you know?"

Flyte had a funny sad little grin on his face. "It told me so."

Kip started to laugh but stopped at the look on his friend's face. "You're serious."

Flyte nodded his head slowly. "I'm serious." He got up suddenly. "So let's just forget the whole thing. Let's go to The Oyster and see how Red's doing."

Kip grabbed him by the shoulder. "You can't leave me just hanging like this, Flyte. You've got to tell me what you're talking about."

"I can't tell you." Flyte's gaze turned inward, as if he were trying to come to a difficult decision. "All I can do is show you."

"Well, show me then."

Flyte started back toward the device. "Plug in, then."

Not sure he was doing the right thing, trembling a little inside, Kip plugged himself into the rig. Even though it was still connected to the wall, nothing happened. "Nothing's happening." He looked at the wall plug. "What do I do?"

"I've got it controlled through my synths." Flyte Error unplugged himself, which made Kip nervous. "Just a mike." He left the room, leaving Kip to get even more nervous about the whole situation. What was he getting himself into? Maybe Red Green had the right idea after all.

Flyte returned with Kip's autar and gave it to him. "If you get into any trouble, just pluck one of the strings. I think I can fix it so that will take you out of the loop."

"What kind of trouble?"

"I can't explain but you'll know it when you see it." He plugged himself back in. "Ready?"

Kip took a deep breath. Flyte's seriousness was making him even more nervous and frightened about what exactly lay ahead for him. "As ready as I'll ever be, I guess."

Flyte Error punched a button on his keyboard and a series of images superimposed themselves on Kip's sight at the same time that the buzzing of a multitude of voices assaulted his hearing.

"Concentrate," Flyte said, both vocally and in Kip's mind. "Pick something to concentrate on and I'll try to follow you."

Kip tried to concentrate on the 'quiste tuft who had been at their performance at the Money Marriage but nothing happened.

Concentrate on Kip Marten. The thought cut through Kip's consciousness. He thought about himself and immediately he was inundated with data about his life, pages full of information—dates and measurements and evaluations—while a voice in his ear recited the same info. A ten-year-old virtual Kip Marten sat in class with Flyte Error and Red Green—Kip reached for the image and suddenly his mind was lost in a kaleidoscopic binary world where data shifted around him in dizzying swirls that confused him until he had forgotten how to get back to himself. He flew down aisles of numbers, spun through case histories and coded graphics, afraid to touch anything, suddenly worried if somehow the squids were recording his passage. He was tossed here and there, first to a factory floor then into a studio then into people's homes, sights and sounds and even odors flickering past him faster than he could comprehend. *Concentrate* Flyte's voice said in his head, *the computer's multitasking and our brains are far too slow to follow it. If you concentrate, it will filter out other information.* He felt Flyte's hand on his back, guiding him, and slowly, though it was measured in nanoseconds, he learned to decelerate and navigate. Flyte showed him how to choose the data pathways to follow, how to interpret the graphics and data files, until at last he hovered over a maze of communication networks, studying it until the pathways made some kind of sense. He sampled them carefully, watching holoshows in progress, spying on programmers editing the shows, and seeing couples on couches, watching HV or not, engrossed in their own concerns, until at last he came to the realization that he was undetected by any of them. He remembered what Flyte had said and strummed a chord on his autar and found himself back in the old warehouse with Flyte.

"What happened?" he asked.

"You were inside the computer. I mean, really inside the computer, Kip. This wasn't like when we were in school."

Kip stood up shakily and began pacing. "What do you mean?"

"When we were in school, all we could do was what the computer let us do. But, with this thing, we go inside the computer and we control it, rather than it controlling us."

"But wasn't that what you did when you found Red and me?"

"I just made some queries and worked my way around some passwords and found out where you guys lived. It was kind of funny, in a way—we lived so close to each other but we never crossed a few streets to look for other people."

"I'll never forget when we found Red."

Red had been on top of a pile of rubble, and other kids were trying to bring him down, using anything they could find, rocks, pieces of concrete. Inevitably he was toppled, blood streaming from his head, but he had been on top of the pile much longer than anybody else had. Although Kip had been stunned when Flyte had found him, Red just took it in stride. "Where you guys been so long?" he asked. They had walked to the foot of the wall and stared up at it, vowing to live there some day, then Red had taken out a penknife and they had cut themselves and mingled blood.

"For life." They had stood a long moment, their hands clasped into one knot, blood streaming down their entangled arms. "Together."

"This is something different, Kip. I went into the spaceship lab before you came back and I found out what it is and the other stuff that we found at Kandalis last night. This is what they were going to use to navigate the starship, a bunch of people all linked together through the computer. None of that 'Spaceshift twelve, Captain' shit. This is a really powerful instrument."

Kip couldn't argue with that, but said, "I don't know, Flyte. This could destroy us. What if they find we've got this thing?"

"We'll be careful. Just one step at a time. And leave ourselves a quick exit, if we can."

And that was the catch, for they had no idea yet what was

possible. "I don't like it," Kip said.

"This could be our mealticket, Kip, our way out of the barraque."

"Or it could be a one-way ticket to The Tower. What are we going to tell Red? You know how he feels about puters."

"We don't tell him nothing. If he finds out about it, then everybody in the barraque will know and we'll be in really deep shit."

"We're in pretty deep shit right now." Flyte said nothing. "And what was that thing doing in the Kandalis refuse bin? Don't tell me someone threw it there by accident."

"The way I figure it, Kip, is that whoever put it there planned to retrieve it before the scavenger truck came."

"Which means they're mad as hell and will kill us to get it back from us." This was one of those situations where there were circles within circles within circles and they were in way over their heads. Kip thought of all the things that could happen to them if they were found with the device in their possession. The smartest thing they could do would be to get rid of it, destroy it.

And yet it beckoned to him and he wanted to put it back on and dive into that binary sea of data, exploring and learning. And if there was anyone who could get them through alive and whole, it was Flyte.

"Tell you what. Let's just go in a couple more times, learn whatever we can, then get rid of it. It's just too damn dangerous to hang on to."

Flyte smiled sadly. "You been readin' my mind, Kip. But I really hate to give it up. Just think of the things we can do. I bet I can get that topside ban changed. If we're careful, we can be fixed for life."

"Fixed? Isn't that what they do to dogs and cats?"

Lady Madonna's girl was standing in the shadows of a

doorway when Casey went out the back door. On the second floor of an old building, the broken glass of one of the windows went up at an angle, looking like the blade of a guillotine. Casey slowly and carefully moved down the alley and came up behind her. He put a hand on her shoulder. "You ought to go home to The Lady now, little one. She'll be angry with you."

She hastily came to her feet.

"What? But you . . . " She looked helplessly toward The Oyster.

"There's usually more than one entrance to a building, little one. You should know that."

"I . . . I didn't know . . . "

"That I knew you were following me? Better people than you have followed me, little one, and I've lost them. Do you wish me to walk you home to The Lady?"

"No, I . . . "

"She won't know."

"I would tell her."

"Of course you would. You're a good little one. But you'd better go. I'm not going to leave until you do." He leaned against the building and watched as Bluebird got up and slowly walked away, looking behind her as she did. He remained leaning against the building. She turned the corner and looked back suddenly. He waved to her.

As Poley passed Tattletale's, a man came out and said, "There's a phone call for you."

He went in but the tender told him that the call had been about half an hour earlier. "It was Walston. He said you should call him back."

Poley was furious. Everyone in the barraque knew that he worked for Walston but they also knew that he played both ends against the middle, that he watched out for Poley first of all, so it was always good to stay on good terms with him. They humored him, they were afraid of him. But for Walston to leave a message for him at Tattletale's so blatantly was pushing the envelope too much. It could cause him a lot of trouble.

He flung open the door to his room, slammed it shut, walked into the convenience, grabbed a bottle, and took a quick hit from it. He had to get control of himself. He couldn't let Walston catch him like this. He took a couple of deep breaths, feeling the liquor fire its way down his throat, ending in a warm coal in his stomach. He waited for it to subside.

He took out his most vicious-looking knife and started peeling an onion, popping the pieces one by one into his mouth. Only when he had calmed down did he finally call Walston. Behind the secretary, the frozen figure of Stefan Coldrider, star of Children of the Undercity, waited for the PLAY command to be given. Poley smiled—who would have thought Walston would be a fan of that drivel? It was another weakness that Poley might be able to exploit some day and it helped to calm him down even more. As Poley had expected, the look on Walston's face told him that the secretary did not enjoy watching someone eating a dirt-grown vegetable instead of the sterile tasteless crap he undoubtedly ate himself.

"It's about time you called, Poley."

Poley was pleased to hear the irritation in Walston's voice. He carefully put the knife down on the table and looked at his employer. "Mister Secretary, don't ever, ever leave a message for me with anyone but Skarys unless I tell you to. This could cost me a lot of trouble."

"This is something out of the ordinary, Poley. Desperate times call for desperate measures."

"You're the one who's desperate, Mister Secretary, not me. But you could make me desperate, and don't forget that desperate men do desperate things." Poley took a long pull from his bottle.

"Are you ready to listen to me, Poley?"

"Go ahead."

Behind Walston, Stefan Coldrider suddenly came to life

for the briefest of moments then froze again. It was probably a programming glitch but Poley filed it away for some possible future use. Right now he had more important things to worry about.

Walston took a deep breath and glared at Poley. "I want you to find someone for me." Poley waited, not giving Walston the pleasure of a response. "His name is Marshall Polansky."

Poley almost choked on his onion. "Polansky? Excuse me, Mister Secretary, but have you gone out of your freakin' mind, sir? Polansky's an old man."

"So am I, Poley. So am I. The computer has identified Polansky as one of the thieves. His DNA was found at the starship lab. Find him and bring him to the police station in Westmeat."

Poley smiled and shook his head. "Who would have thought that of the old man? Well, well, well. But I can't bring him to you. That's going too far. You'll have to send one of your own men. I'll find out where he is and let you know."

"You have the tranks I gave you several months ago?"

Poley hesitated a moment. "Yes."

"Get Polansky and bring him to the top of the wall."

"But can't you find him through his tracer? Surely he had one put in him when he left The Tower."

"That was over fifty years ago. Its battery ran down long ago. It lasted a lot longer than some of those we've used recently."

Poley recognized the not-so-veiled threat—Poley had dealt with his own tracer several years earlier. He had found a tech who could alter it so that it began operating erratically until it finally quit working completely after several months.

"Mister Secretary, going openly to the police would compromise me so much I might be useless to you in the future."

"I'm not interested in the future right now. Bring him to the station. And Poley . . . " He waited until he was certain he had Poley's attention. "In the future, just leave your message with the computer. There is no need to disturb me."

"As you wish, Mr. Secretary." There was no sense in reminding Walston that he was the one who had asked Poley to call him.

Walston broke the connection before Poley could make any more objections.

How was he going to get out of this one? He had always managed to steer clear of dealing with the police directly and now Walston was putting him on the line.

Poley put his knife and half-eaten onion away and took a good healthy drink from what was left in his bottle from the night before and went out to find the old man.

"Ready?" Flyte asked.

"I guess so." Kip had his autar and Flyte his synthkeys.

"Okay. Now, listen, you've got to stick with me. I know how to handle this thing better than you do. Okay? I've got more experience. It won't be difficult. They've engineered this thing so that people can work together on it."

"How do you know all this stuff?"

"I've been doing it all my life, while you and Red were chasing tuft. And I was in the file that described what it does. I know, Kip."

"Okay. Let's fly."

They dove in recklessly, swimming toward their data files, floating in a lake of information, numerous photofiles of themselves at various times in their lives, some holo, some flat, arrest records and (surprise!) a number of incidents when they had escaped arrest. Their parents and pointers to their files, known addresses, current address (how did they know?), intelligence and emotional quotients at various times in his life, psychological profiles and updates. Kip felt pride at his IQ and the comments about it and took umbrage at the psych-file that said he was unstable and lacked motivation. What did they know about motivation? He lacked their idea of motivation. Who wanted to work as a compjock for some warehouse in the barraque all his life?

They traced the cred pointers back to the main directory and transferred additional credit to Flyte's file, Red's, and Kip's. *This is child's play,* Flyte transmitted. *It's a lot easier than stealing moments from a club's puter while you and Red try to keep the club manager from noticing.* Here they had easy access not only to the cred files but to any other files they wanted to trace, and all the time in the world, in a world where time was measured in picoseconds.

He felt, saw, smelled, heard, tasted the city, all around him and part of him. He flashed on and off, directing traffic as he himself was directed by sensing devices. He looked through a dozen lenses into the streets of topside, watching people streaming through a dozen different forms of pleasure. And through the personal terminals of its many inhabitants, even the terminals that were turned off, he watched the citizens at home, watching HV, playing, working, making love.

And then he found himself soaring over the barraque, looking down, searching for something. *What are you?* he asked the puter and the puter replied, *I am a Speye*, and in a nanosecond Flyte knew everything about them, how they were sent down to the barraque every night, watching from overhead, clinging to buildings and listening to secret conversations. He remembered how he and his friends had stoned one on one of those rare occasions when they were sent during the day and they didn't know what it was but they didn't like it for some reason and now he knew everything about them, how they were used all the time topside but were rarely sent to the barraque during the day because so many had been destroyed.

Something flashed by at the periphery of Kip's awareness and, without thinking, he was dragged after it. For a long moment measured in miniseconds, he panicked, thinking that they had been detected, then he relaxed as he realized that it was his own mind that had followed the data, alerted by the fact that it was a high priority, as high a priority could be without being a danger interrupt.

What *is* this? he asked Flyte.

They were between the two ends of a commcall. At one end, Poley was cutting pieces of an onion with a vicious-looking knife and popping the peelings into his mouth. He was a small man, wiry, sleepy-eyed, with a weak chin and an easy smile.

"I've been talking with Skarys," Poley said as he put another peeling into his mouth, "and he will look into things tonight."

"I'm not asking for information tonight or tomorrow," the other man, who was considerably older and quite stocky, snapped. "I want it now."

Kip wanted to ask Flyte if he knew who the other man was but he was afraid that they would hear him.

"Perhaps we should restrict the access the barraquistes have to the city."

What? The man was not a 'quiste . . . which meant he had to be Poley's boss, Benj Walston, Secretary of Security. Kip was torn between the fascination of listening to the two men and the need to strum his autar and break the connection with the puter.

Poley laughed. "That might not be a bad idea. Then the 'quistes would riot and you'd have plenty of reason to keep them down for a long, long time."

"And I'd be out loading trucks with you and your friends. No thank you, Poley."

Walston seemed to be staring right at Kip, sending an icicle of fear into him. But Walston ignored him, as if he didn't see him. Suddenly feeling like a minor god, Kip turned on the Stefan Coldrider HV behind Walston but a millisecond later thought better of it and turned it off again.

"One other thing. I tried to recruit Red Green but he was cold to the idea. Nonetheless I think he'll come round in time."

No! Not Red! Of all the people Kip knew, Red was the last one he could think of who would work for Walston.

Walston glared at Poley. "I want you to find someone for me." Poley said nothing. "His name is Marshall Polansky."

Poley finally lost his composure, nearly choking on a piece of onion.

"Find him and bring him to the top of the wall."

As soon as the connection was broken, Kip immediately strummed a chord on his autar and found himself back in the abandoned factory. He looked over at Flyte, who seemed to be still inside the puter. "Flyte? Flyte?" He felt close to panic and he needed the reassurance of his bandmate's knowledge and calm.

Flyte reached out and touched his synthkeys then looked at Kip with eyes that were still a little glazed.

"Do you know what that was all about?" The panic Kip felt was in his voice.

Flyte Error got up and began pacing the room, as he usually did when he was trying to think things through. "That was Secretary Walston and Poley."

"I figured that out but what were they talking about?"

Flyte looked out one of the windows. "I don't know." It was mostly darkness out there now except for a few small fires where the homeless gathered. "But one thing's for sure. We've always stayed out of Poley's path but we've got to be even more careful from now on. He's even more dangerous than I thought."

"But what about Red? And Marshall Polansky?"

Flyte Error smiled. "Marshall Polansky. The Polish Avenger."

Years ago, long before Kip and Flyte and Red had been born, Marshall Polansky had taken part in an uprising in the barraque, calling himself The Polish Avenger. The name had stuck to him as a mark of derision and ridicule and made him a laughing-stock in the barraque.

"I don't know. Walston must have gone gonzo if he's spiking Marshall Polansky."

"And Red?"

Flyte's face turned hard. "I told you not to trust him."

"But we're blood!" Kip protested. "That's more important

to Red than it is to us!"

"You heard what Poley said. If Red got a chance to jump to another band, I'd bet he'd take it."

Kip shook his head. "Not Red. I can't believe Red would do something like that."

"We're just going to have to keep an eye on him from now on. And this is another reason not him to let him know about this thing."

"Sure, sure." It was just so hard to believe. Red Green, of all people. And Walston, Poley, and Marshall Polansky. It didn't make any sense at all. "Think we should warn Polansky?"

Flyte took a moment to think about it. "And cross Poley? I'd like to, Kip, but it's just too damn dangerous."

Kip agreed with him but it still didn't seem right. "Maybe we can find a way to tell him without mentioning Poley."

"Sure. And maybe we'll be HV stars next week. We don't even know where to find him. There's something else, Kip." Kip looked at his friend, wondering what confusing new information he was about hear. "While we were listening to them, I was able to get access to Walston's files and I stored them in a private file of my own."

"You've gone gonzo yourself, Flyte. What if Walston finds out?"

"He can't. I erased all the access paths. I'm the only one who knows about it. Even the puter itself doesn't know about it. I'm the only one now who can access that file." Flyte walked back to the device. "I've got to go back in."

"No!" Kip tried to calm himself. "We're already in enough trouble."

"That's why I've got to go back. I need to make sure there's nothing there that can be traced back to us. You don't have to come with me."

"We're blood." Kip thought he sounded like Red Green.

This time it took only a few mikes to get oriented. Kip followed Flyte carefully as he explored the city, going down avenues and into restaurants and theatres and showplaces where they had never been and never would have been allowed. They were the traffic controller in the center of the city; they were eyes that spied through hundreds of HVs, whether or not they had been activated. They were everywhere; they were omniscient. Wherever Flyte turned his attention, they would be there. They had become gods, minor gods perhaps, only city gods, but gods nonetheless and it was intoxicating.

Flyte found the file on the band and changed its entry from Banned From Performing in the Zone to Take Care in Hiring. *If that doesn't draw attention,* he said, *I'll upgrade it later.*

Kip's concentration faltered a moment and he felt himself drawn to something that looked like a red door to him. Abandon hope, all you who enter, the door said but somehow Kip knew it was where all the secrets were hidden, all the information and knowledge that they needed.

"Kip!" Flyte said, but Kip was already through the door.

She barely heard Bluebird when she entered. It had all been too easy. The data was spread out there in front of her as if it had always been there. And yet it couldn't have been. She could not have been that blind. She was getting old, caught up with her own concerns, her aging body, her customers . . . no! her own concerns were the barraque and its people. She should have seen it before; she would have seen it. The data had been hidden before but now it was as if the computer knew that she already suspected and the knowledge could no longer be hidden from her. But how could he have known so quickly?

"Lady?"

"Where have you been, child?" She tried to put a bit of anger into her voice but her heart wasn't in it. She noticed that Bluebird had noticed it as well. "Go heat up something to eat, girl."

"Is something wrong, Lady?"

"It does not concern you, child."

"Everything concerns me, Lady. You've told me that often enough."

Lady Madonna smiled in spite of herself. "Sometimes you learn your lessons too well, child, and always the ones I wish you wouldn't. Go eat. Perhaps we'll talk of it later."

The girl started to leave but stopped in the doorway. "Oh, I saw the old lady on the square this morning. She said to tell you that Gloria says the night is coming."

Lady Madonna smiled. "Of course."

"Do you know what that means?"

"It means . . . it could mean trouble. Many things are coming to a head. Go eat, child. I need to be alone. I need to think."

"Yes, Lady," Bluebird said meekly and left. The Lady smiled again. A year earlier, the girl would have fought like an alley cat to find out what she wanted to know. Everything had been a frontal assault. She had since learned the price of impatience and the value of moving around the edges, coming from unexpected sides. Unless she had become meekness itself and that was extremely unlikely. "Where were you all day, girl?" The Lady muttered to herself.

But that was the least of her worries. The Night was coming. She had been looking forward to it, as she always did, when she could still revel in her voice, when the whole barraque held its breath to hear her voice, and this time Bluebird would share in her triumph. But this time there was an ugliness that could turn the night into bitterness, into fire and blood. That must not be. If only Tor could tell her what to do.

She turned to her console and began typing rapidly. Voice commands were impressive and worked well for ordinary chores but nothing could match the precision and clarity of typed commands. One could review them and shape them. That Bluebird could not hear them was an added bonus.

Some day she'd have to teach the girl this too but she was still a long way from being ready for it. Well, at her age, Lady Madonna hadn't been ready either.

She called up a new file, marked it, and fed it the data she had been reading all afternoon then added the news that the Night was coming. The computer queried for a more specific time period. After thinking a while, she fed it a 5 and appended a ? to the data. She called up a group profile analysis program and fed it the data, marked everything Personal Confidential, and began reviewing the data while waiting for the program's conclusions.

"What are you doing, Lady?"

Lady Madonna twitched a little. She had been so engrossed in her work that she hadn't heard Bluebird return to the room.

"I've never seen you so worried."

She sat back and smiled at the girl. "Sit down, Bluebird. No, you've never seen me so worried because I haven't been this worried in quite a long time."

"Is it the Night?"

"No. That only complicates matters."

"She meant svana, didn't she?"

"How long did it take you figure that out?"

"Not very. But how does she know?"

"She is head of one of the proudest and most powerful families in the barraque."

"Then why does she sit in the square all the time like that?"

"Why not? It's warm, it's safe, and there's no better place to learn all the news and gossip."

"I don't understand."

"Maybe if you get to be as old as her, you will. But if you continue to carouse till all hours of the night and get involved in brawls in the upper city, you won't live to see the next svana."

"It will be soon, won't it?"

"You already know more than you should, child."

"I know enough to keep quiet and enough to be ready for it when it comes."

"Are you?"

"I will be. You've taught me . . . "

(53)

"Oh, yes, I've taught you many things but what have you learned? You haven't even done your scales today, child. Go and warm up your voice. I'll be with you soon and we can practice together."

Lady Madonna sighed as she watched the girl leave and turned back to the computer. The profile analysis was done—it was reassuring. The trends that Casey George had brought to her attention would not affect much of anything in the barraque for several months.

But what if the trends accelerated? She would have to worry about that later, after giving Bluebird her latest vocal lesson. "Sometimes I wish I felt no more than you," she said to the computer. It said nothing back.

The man had been convicted of a brutal rape. Now he himself was raped and sodomized several times a day in the prison of his mind. Kip pulled back in horror and, for a year of picoseconds, he stared at the prisoner through the monitor circuits, strapped to a bed, twitching and moaning. He knew everything that was happening inside the man's mind. A few days of this, perhaps less, and he would be released, broken and harmless, hypnotic commands implanted to bring these mental experiences back to the surface if he should even contemplate another crime.

In another room, a young woman felt the pain of being murdered in the same grisly fashion in which she had killed several other people. Did it matter what they had done to her that caused her to retaliate in such a grim and final fashion?

What is crime? A young boy, only a few years younger than Kip himself, lay in another room, suffering because he had stolen some food. How can you punish hunger? By mentally chopping off his fingers every time he reaches for something that doesn't belong to him? The price was far beyond the act, even if the torture left no physical scars, only mental ones.

And there were the files, of every inhabitant of The Tower for over a hundred years. Some of the names were familiar to Kip, although he'd never met them: China Leonard, Marshall Polansky, Maggie Mandolin, others. He sought out the hidden file in The Tower's binary runes that contained all the information on Benj Walston, seeking the knowledge that could destroy him.

And he found very little.

As far as the puter was concerned, Benj Walston had been born a grown man, making his debut as a minor city functionary and working his way upward and inward until he became Security itself, inheriting the mantle of those who had persecuted China Leonard and Marshall Polansky. Those were not his doing but there were still many lesser people, whose crimes had been those of hope and despair, whom Benj Walston had quite willingly tormented in The Tower until they were ready to act in whatever manner Benj Walston and the city wanted them to act.

But there was no trace of Benj Walston's origins, thoroughly erased by Walston himself, no doubt, and altered electrons leave no traces, no faint scribblings on the paper underneath. The records might be offline, in some rotting tapes or disks, inaccessible to the puter and therefore inaccessible to Kip Marten.

His anger was ebbing as his fear returned. After all, what could he do? He was just a barraquiste musician who had stumbled onto something that was light-years beyond him. If Walston found out he was here, spying on him and the city, the price for him would be The Tower.

He started to leave but found his way blocked by a presence of some kind, an amorphous black blob that seemed to radiate animosity. *Identify!* it demanded.

Identify? He was trapped. He did not belong here. The walls were moving in on him. Flyte! There were manacles on the walls that would tie him down forever, while he was tortured mentally in some way that he couldn't begin to imagine. Flyte! Help me! There was no escape. Soon he would be crushed to death by the walls. Would his virtual death be echoed by the physical death of his body? There was nothing in Kip's experience that told him what would happen to him or how he could escape it.

Kip. He heard Flyte's voice from a distance. A, Kip, B-seven.

A, B-seven. For a nanosecond, Kip wondered why Flyte wanted him to think about music but he had to trust his friend. Only Flyte could help him; only Flyte had the experience and the knowledge. What was next? One, four, five. A, B-seven. . .

Kip found himself back in a concrete-walled room in an empty building in the warehouse section of the barraque, his body seeming to vibrate with the E chord he had just strummed. One (E), four (A), five (B-seven), and back to the major chord, E. The room was cold but it seemed even colder to him, a chill that went to the very core of his body. Kip Marten had been frightened many times in his short life but he had never approached being this terrified. He felt weak and wanted to be sick.

"You okay, Kip?" Flyte was already standing next to him, looking down at him.

"I think so. I just . . . Lord!" He put his head in his hands.

"For a while there, I thought I'd lost you. I wasn't sure you'd be able to get back."

"But that . . . that thing! It knows I was there. It'll come after me."

"It was just a puter program, Kip. As soon as you disappeared from The Tower, it forgot all about you and went back to guarding. It's okay."

"You're sure?"

"Yeah. I checked before I came back here."

"Hey, anybody home?" They both turned around at the sound of Red's voice. He walked through the doorway and looked around at the scattered electronic parts. "What a mess! Remind me never to marry you, Flyte."

"Are you okay, Red?" Kip asked.

"Sure. Why shouldn't I be?" Red let out a belch.

"You're drunk," Flyte accused.

"That's why I'm okay. What've you two been up to?"

"Nothing much," Flyte said.

"We've been trying to figure out what this new toy of Flyte's does," Kip said.

"Yeah. What does it do?"

They were quiet for a moment until at last Flyte said, "Not much. It's been a waste of time."

Red laughed then belched again. "Better your time than mine. You guys should go out drinking more. You're too damn serious." He stretched broadly and yawned. "See you in the morning."

As he left the room, Kip and Flyte looked at each other. "Let's close things down," Flyte said.

Marshall Polansky was not difficult to find. All one had to do was search the bars of the barraque. That was an equation that would work for eighty or ninety percent of the barraquistes and it worked for Marshall Polansky. Poley found him in the seventh bar he tried, the lucky seventh. Of course, it wasn't pure luck by any means. There were more than seven bars in the barraque, lots more, but Poley knew the favorite bars of many of the barraquistes and Skarys knew most of the rest. Poley prided himself on the notion that he could locate any barraquiste within an hour and, although that may not have been strictly true, he had yet to fail whenever such a mission became necessary.

Polansky was in the middle of a group of men in the middle of a go game so Poley ordered a bottle and sat back in a corner to watch and wait for his moment. There had been a time when he had been quick and anxious, nervous and always looking for action, not unlike Red Green and his friends, but those days were gone, long gone. The Tower had taken much of it out of him. He hadn't spent much time there, less than a week, but subjectively it had been years and had aged him way beyond his years. Still, he could be quick when he needed to be.

His irritation at Walston nettled him and made him impatient when he should be just sitting back and letting things come to him, flowing with the action instead of trying to force it. He had to be careful; Poley knew the price of impatience. But Walston was impatient too and Poley wondered why. This was not the usual harassment to which Walston subjected him and the rest of the barraquistes. Something important was happening and Poley was annoyed that he didn't know what it was. There was supposed to have been a raid tonight on some of the plotters and trouble-makers but it hadn't happened. Poley was certain that Walston had cancelled it himself.

Marshall Polansky left the go game and moved toward the bar. Poley moved quickly to his side.

"Let me buy this one for you, Marsh."

"I can still buy m'own liquor," the old man said. "I don't need none of yours."

"Just trying to be friendly."

"Whenever you're friendly, Poley, someone's in trouble."

"I'm always friendly."

"Yeah? Well, someone's always in trouble."

"That someone wouldn't be you, would it?"

"Me? I got no trouble I never had before. I've had trouble all m'life and tonight's no different."

"I hear you had a little trouble last night."

"Yeah? What'd you hear?" Something flickered briefly behind the old man's eyes. Fear? Anger?

"That you were someplace you weren't supposed to be." It was a guess, but a good one, knowing that Walston wanted Polansky and that Walston was worried about the break-in.

"Who told you that?"

"You went topside last night, didn't you?"

"I ain't sayin' nothin'."

"Don't matter none to me. Just thought I'd give you a friendly warning, that's all. I'd go rabbit if I were you, before the squids come lookin'."

Polansky was still trying to bluff it out but Poley could see the panic in his eyes. He'd struck home and placed his dart where he'd wanted it. He left the bar, never turning around to look back at Polansky, who was probably still standing there, dumbstruck. He crossed the street and walked halfway down the block before he dared to glance behind him. Polansky was standing uncertainly in the doorway of the bar.

Poley kept going and turned the corner. He crossed the street again and looked back. Polansky was going in the opposite direction. Poley followed, keeping to the shadows as if he were one of them. It probably wasn't necessary—Poley was certain that one of Walston's spy machines was following both of them. The knowledge, however, wasn't particularly comforting. He wished that he had an ear with him but that would have been certain poison in the barraque. Besides, then he would have had to put up with Walston's irritating commands.

"No way, no way, no way! You're not going to electrocute me with that thing! If I'm going to die, then I want it to be nice and clean . . . "

"Nothing's cleaner than electricity," Kip said.

"A knife thrust to the heart. That's the way I want to go."

"Spare us the phony melodramatics," Flyte Error said.

"Or punched and kicked and beaten to death by a frenzied mob of sex-starved virgins!"

Kip and Flyte Error grabbed Red's arms and tried to hold him down but it was futile. He thrust them aside as if they were a pair of cockroaches.

"I thought we were blood!" he roared. "Blood, sperm, and guts! Together forever."

"Lord, Red, we're only trying to show you something!" Kip nursed the back of his hand, which had been skinned when Red had thrust him away and was oozing blood.

"You can't show me nothing, you little pansies! You guys'd be nothing without me!"

"But, look, you saw what we . . . "

"I saw two assholes sitting around looking silly with straps on their heads, making weird little comments and staring at something that wasn't even there."

Kip grinned at Red. "Hell, I've seen you stare at things that weren't there lots of times."

"And tried to brush them off your clothes like they were on fire," Flyte Error added.

"That's different. I had good reason. I didn't see you guys drinkin' or sniffin' or patchin' nothin'. You're straight and sober as a topside judge, plugged into the flippin' wall like some compjock, starin' at somethin' that ain't even there and gabblin' away this gibberish about concentration and there it is, do you see it?"

"Ah, forget about him, Flyte. He's chicken."

"Damn straight I'm chicken. You ain't gonna get me on that one, Kip. I'm too keen for you. I don't go around stickin' my finger into lectric sockets just for the hell of it. I may be dumb but I ain't stupid."

"Maybe we should rehearse then."

"You guys rehearse. You need it. Me, all I got is my voice and it don't need no rehearsal. It just needs rest."

"I don't hear you restin' it none," Flyte said moodily.

"I'm gonna rest it down at the Oyster in a jar of their finest."

"Don't do no patchin'."

But Flyte's comment was to Red's back as he walked out the doorway and left them alone in the old abandoned factory. Flyte looked at Kip. "Ain't you goin' with him?"

"Nah. Let him go. You got any gigs on line for us?"

"I'm workin' on a few but they're all down here in the barraque."

"Red ain't gonna like that. He likes spiffy tuft."

"Well, it's his own damn fault. We ain't getting' nothing topside for a while, not after that drag-outer at the Money Marriage. We is tabu topside, sahib."

"You want to try practicin' with that rig of yours, see if it will work the way you think it will?"

"No. Not yet. I've got a few things I want to work out on it yet. Keep an eye on Red, follow him. Like you said, he's our ticket and we gotta keep him laundered."

"You sure?" Kip looked at Flyte Error, uncertain.

"Yeah. Unless you wanna sit around here and watch me play with screwdrivers and pliers and probes."

"I was hopin' maybe we could see some more HV."

"Go down to the Oyster."

"Ah, it's not the same."

"Later, Kip, after I work some things out, okay?"

"Sure." Kip left but he was still uncertain. Usually Flyte Error was happy to have him around and tried to get him to stay. It was unusual for him to want to be alone. But maybe he really was on to something. He wouldn't stay long at the Oyster, just a long sniff or two, then he'd come back and see what Flyte was up to.

Poley was getting frustrated. Marsh was entering bar after bar but not staying long in any of them. Obviously he was looking for someone but who? There wasn't time to go into a bar and find out, not if he was to stay on Polansky's trail. Walston undoubtedly was watching all this with one of his flying spy machines, unable to contact Poley, and the thought of Walston's frustration kept Poley amused and smiling. But he didn't even have time for a drink. He kicked at a mangy dog he passed in the street but the wary dog was too far away.

At last Poley was able to step into a bar across the street from one that Polansky had entered. There was an old beat-up pubcomm near the front window; Poley punched in his credcode and the number of the bar where Skarys was working. He waited impatiently until the bouncer came on line.

"Nick. Listen carefully. You know Marshall

Polansky?"

"Yeah, sure. Listen, I got to get back to work."

"He's going around all the bars looking for someone. I'm tailing him and I can't take time to find out who he's asking for. See if you can find out."

"Listen, Poley, I can't . . . "

"I'll call you back next chance I get."

Polansky was on the prowl again. Poley hung up and started out the door. A hairy hand fell on his shoulder. Poley turned to see a gorilla looking back at him.

"You drink. You buy."

Poley looked up at the gorilla. This was no time to argue. He stalked over to the bar and shoved his credcard at the tender. "Gimme a beer." The price didn't matter right now. The tender took his own sweet time drawing it. Poley grabbed it and walked over to the gorilla. "Here," he said, "this is for you." He doused the gorilla with the beer and walked out. He had lost precious seconds with that act but he got out on the street just in time to see Polansky enter a bar ten doors down.

Nighttime slipped over the barraque in barely perceptible phases. Instead of falling down from the sky, it seemed to ooze out of the cracks in the streets, moving its way up the battered buildings, crawling up the ancient rock wall that towered over the barraque, separating it from the upper city, which was still bathed in sunlight even as lights began to flicker on hesitantly below, where the river coursed in its sluggish and multi-colored current, loaded with its freight of waste chemicals and sludge.

It seemed as if every other building in the barraque was a bar or tavern or some other establishment designed to help the barraquistes forget their lives and instead rejoice in their own camaraderie and togetherness, fragile though that might be. In one tavern, known only as The Oyster (and few in the barraque had any idea what an Oyster was, had been, or was supposed to be), a group met with irregular regularity in the back room, raising the sound level higher and higher until anyone who did not belong to the group and who had the temerity to sit in the back room would be driven out.

Green smiled as he walked into the back room of The Oyster. They were all here, or most of them, the young musicians and artists of the barraque, or at least those whom Green had hung around with at various times in his young life. They ignored the rotting and decaying carpet, the lack of ventilation, because it had the cheapest prices in Westmeat. There was Brooky, with dark wild hair and a scraggly beard, whose body sometimes jerked like a puppet controlled by an epileptic puppeteer. There was Morrisdaughter, cute and vivacious Morrisdaughter, with a mouth that would have embarrassed a stevedore in times long past. In a corner, Demon Pawn had cornered Libido and was trying to impress her with his knowledge of HV trivia, despite the fact that he had failed in hundreds of previous attempts with her and other tufts. And so it went down in the back room of The Oyster, nearly a dozen conversations going on simultaneously, overlapping and interacting with each other, Radish jumping from one to another as a comment caught her attention, from Eden to The Old Man Himself, coughing and sniffing, up to the front to get refreshers, liquids and munchies and sniffers and once in while a patch, which the others would pretend they hadn't seen, their uncomfortability with a patcher quickly forgotten in their conversations.

The Old Man Himself looked up as Green came in then looked away. Meanwhile Radish moved over to him and embraced him. "Hey, stud, where ya been?'

Green grinned and grabbed himself a squeeze. Radish squealed and moved away but not far. "Around. Y'hear what happened last night?"

"Hear? I was there. We all were."

Green looked at The Old Man Himself."All of you?"

"Well, almost all."

"I hear you ain't playing topside no more," Brooky said,

moving into the conversation with a smoothness that belied his occasional jerky clumsiness.

"Where y'hear that?"

"Around. The top squids have banned you guys."

"We'll be back. Can't keep a good band down."

"Yeah," Brooky said grumpily, "but they're banning all of us. It's not just you. No 'quiste bands topside. That's the rule now. You've bummed it for all of us."

Red held up his hands. "Not to worry. Times change. They always do. The topside tufts and dudes will complain to their mommies and daddies and next thing you know we'll be topside again."

"Sure," Brooky said bleakly.

Green became aware of a sudden silence in the conversations in The Oyster's back room and turned around to see Casey George in the doorway. Once Casey had been in the very center of the group but now he was part of something else and that made them all nervous. They had all thought he could have been an HV star. Even now his face had a kind of craggy handsomeness through its weariness, and his body was still hard and lean. If he was a heavy patcher, as was rumored, he hadn't let his body down, as so many patchers did.

"Casey!" The Old Man Himself's voice needed no amplification. He had almost been an HV star himself once long ago, so it was rumored. "Sit down, sit down. It's good to see you again."

Casey grinned, a boyish grin that turned that hard-bitten face into that of a child. "Sorry I haven't been around. I've been busy."

"Of course you have. We all have."

Morrisdaughter sidled up to Casey George. "How ya been? Haven't seen you in a long time. Missed ya."

Casey put an arm around her and fondled her ample breasts. "Too long," he said. "I began to forget what you were like."

"You never forget that," The Old Man Himself said. He reached out and Brooky put a sniffer in his hand. He inhaled deeply then patted Casey George's hand.

Casey grasped The Old Man Himself's hand in his, two large workingmen's hands, one old and gnarled with time and age, the other hard and callused. Nearly identical painful smiles crossed the faces of both men.

"I'm sorry," Casey George said softly. "I've been busy."

"You're here now," The Old Man Himself said. "That's all that matters."

"No, it isn't. Things are happening upstairs."

Brooky sneered. "Things are always happening upstairs."

"But these things are going to affect us. All of us."

"And that's no new truth either. They say one word and the squids all jump to shit and, when they shit, they shit on us and we do our best to duck."

"What's happening this time?" The Old Man Himself asked.

"It's the starship."

"Fuck the starship," Brooky said.

"No, no." Demon Pawn, who had studiously been avoiding Casey George, turned suddenly at mention of the starship. "Let's hear what Casey has to say."

"Demon, my man," Brooky said, "you ain't never going on no starship. They don't take fuckheads."

"That's what you think. I've got plans. I've got dreams."

"Dreams, yes. Dreams and fantasies."

"Will you guys shut up and let Casey speak?" The Old Man Himself roared.

Brooky shrugged and turned his back to them, temporarily blocking the path of an old derelict who had come back to use the men's convenience.

"The starship is finished."

"Are you sure?" Libido asked.

"Shut. Up." The Old Man Himself bit off each word.

"There's a lot of work left to do on it but everything necessary for its trip is done. It could leave tomorrow if necessary. Crew's quarters and stuff like that need to be finished but all the technical work for the trip has been completed."

"That means . . . " The Old Man Himself paused, thoughtful.

There was a moment of silence while everyone followed The Old Man Himself's thoughts, until Demon Pawn said, "Could it be manned as is, without completion of the crew's quarters?"

"How should I know?" Casey George said. "Maybe. I don't know."

"There will be no work for us to do then," The Old Man Himself said softly. "Our jobs are over."

Brooky turned around to look thoughtfully at all of them.

"Soon enough." Casey George stood up. "I've got to go. I have other people to tell."

"You'll tell us as soon as you know anything else?" Brooky said nervously.

"Of course. You're still family."

Then he was gone. Brooky ordered some new sniffers and began inhaling seriously while the others took their own narcotics, depressants, and inhalants.

Several bars later, Casey was talking to several millworkers when Polansky came up behind him. "Casey. Poley said I'm in trouble."

"Yeah? He's just trying to scare you, Marsh."

"No. Listen." When Polansky started to tell Casey what had happened, Casey stopped him and pulled him off in a corner to hear the rest of his tale, convincing Casey that Poley wasn't just fishing for information he could sell to Walston or someone else but knew about the break-in and thought Polansky had something to do with it.

"Okay, Marsh. Here's what you do. You head for our escape route. I'll be right behind you. Okay?"

"Yeah, yeah."

The old man left the bar and Casey called The Oyster. "Is The Old Man there?" Of course he was. He was always at The Oyster. "Tell him I've been delayed." Casey broke the connection and walked out of the bar, knowing that The Old Man Himself would relay the message to Demon Pawn.

Polansky had stopped at the corner of a building then moved on when Casey nodded to him. Casey waited a moment then saw Poley move out of the shadows and follow the old man. When Poley was gone, Casey moved to follow both of them, having no trouble keeping out of sight since he knew exactly where Marsh was going.

Lady Madonna lay down wearily. This was costing her needed sleep. She wanted to work with the computer again but she dared not while Bluebird was home. And tonight, of course, the girl was staying home. They had done their scales, the silly rhymes they used to warm up their voices, practiced trills and all the vocal practices that The Lady could think of, and Bluebird had followed her effortlessly and flawlessly. She herself had felt the strain and had pulled back, as Bluebird herself would some day learn to do. But her voice, as Lady Madonna's had been, was now a faithful and loyal servant and it was clear and crystal and flawless, without strain.

Lady Madonna wanted her to go out and do something, so she could be alone but, after all the lectures she had given to Bluebird about taking care of herself and her voice, she had no choice but to remain silent. It was as if the girl could read her mind and do exactly what Lady Madonna didn't want her to do. She was being hoist on the petard of her own advice and had to remain silent.

The bedside monitor was not sufficiently flexible to do what she needed to do. She had lived alone too long and now she was, in a sense, a prisoner of her own bedroom. If she had put the main computer console here, she could work while the young girl slept. Now, she dared not . . . and yet . . .

Her curiosity got the better of her and she went into the main living area. Bluebird's door was closed. She turned on the console and began typing instructions, activating a worm program she had written long ago and that she used often. At first she had asked it to print out the most often asked-for information but she had been overwhelmed by the data. Now she looked for data that had only been referenced a few times in the past few days, especially that which was rarely referenced at all. Most of the time it was just some student researching some obscure historical information but every once in a while it brought something interesting to her attention.

Tonight it showed several references to Marshall Polansky. Why in the world would anyone be interested in Marshall Polansky? It had been years since anyone other than Marshall himself had referenced his file. There had been many references in the days when he had called himself the Polish Avenger, arrested and sent to The Tower, with follow-ups as authorities checked on his conditioning, checks that had grown fewer and fewer through the years as he grew older and became no longer a threat until they finally completely ceased, as others became more important to them.

Try as she may, she could see nothing in Marshall's file that was suspicious, no extra funds to his account, no observations of being seen in the wrong places with the wrong people, no unaccounted-for absences. He had been a model citizen for nearly the past fifty years, reporting for work regularly, first as a machinist, then as a handler, down the list of jobs requiring less and less strength and agility, until he now was a watchman, still working faithfully at the same place all these years.

Curiosity unfulfilled, she called up Casey George's file. Here was a file filled with incidents and events—none serious enough for more than fines and formal reprimands. And jobs aplenty, from factory to another until . . . three months ago he begun work as a machinist at the same factory where Marshall Polansky had worked all these years. Was it coincidence that brought these two men together at a time when someone was checking on Marshall Polansky's file at the same time that Casey George was paying a mysterious visit to Lady Madonna? She could find no connection between the two men in the computer but Lady Madonna felt certain that the two events were somehow connected.

She turned off the console and returned to bed, still confused and puzzled. Perhaps in the night her subconscious would come up with the answer or at least a clue to it. She never saw Bluebird watching her from the dark of her own room.

Poley waited in the shadows, until he felt he knew every step in the fire escape on the side of the building. Polansky must have found what he wanted in the bar, ChiLil's, and Poley wanted to barge in and learn who Polansky had found. Instead, he moved to a bar on the same side as ChiLil's and punched Skarys's bar again.

After one peremptory ring, the phone was silent in his hand. "Hello?" he asked tentatively.

"Good. It's you." Poley recognized Walston's voice.

"What the hell?"

"Listen. I want Polansky and I want him now. You have the tranks I gave you several months ago?"

"Yes."

"You have them with you?"

Poley thought of lying but decided against it. "Yes."

"Get him and bring him to the top of the wall."

"But . . . "

"Hurry. He just left the bar."

The line went dead and Poley glared at it before hanging up. He went out in time to see Polansky turn a corner. He was no longer looking in practically every bar. He was a man with a mission now, perhaps a scared rat looking for a hiding hole. Poley couldn't grab him openly on the street but in a few minutes they would be in Westmeat. Still Poley couldn't approach him straight on; he couldn't give Polansky time to get ready for him. Things were going too fast; Walston hadn't given him enough time to plan things out carefully. When things got rushed like this, mistakes were made, serious mistakes. Polansky reached a deserted building that Poley knew well. The old man turned the corner at the building as Poley reached the alley on the other side. He went down the alley, nimbly dodging litter and trash as if he could see in the dark. Nonetheless he tripped over a brickbat and stopped, listening, then he stepped into an open doorway and raced across the shadowed floor, carefully avoiding the rotten wood, rusty nails, and broken glass. Through a shattered window he could see Polansky moving swiftly alongside the building. Poley smiled. The timing was going to be right.

He reached the other side of the building, came out of an open doorway as Polansky walked by, stepped up behind him, and slapped the patch on the back of his neck. Polansky turned. "You! What did you . . . ?" He grabbed the patch from his neck as Poley stood there smiling. "What did you . . . ?" he said again, staring in puzzlement at the patch in his hand.

"Come along, Marshall. Come with me." Poley took him firmly by the elbow and they started walking toward the wall.

Polansky smiled innocently. "Where are we going?"

"Don't worry, Marshall . . . " Before he could finish, a blinding pain flashed through Poley's head and the world disappeared until he awoke face down on the wet pavement, his hair matted with his own blood, a splitting headache for a companion, and Marshall Polansky gone.

Casey George hesitated for a moment when Poley darted into a building, trying to decide whether to follow Poley or Polansky, finally keeping a block behind Polansky, seeing Poley come out of the other side of the building and trank the old man.

Moving as softly as he could, Casey moved up quickly. Poley was concentrating too much on keeping Polansky on his feet, and Casey was able to use his blackjack on Walston's agent, then propped up the old man and started steering him further down the street.

"Where we goin'?" the old man mumbled.

"Just keep talkin', Marsh. We're going to be okay soon." Casey thought of using one of his own patches on Polansky but that could easily kill the old man, not a bad idea in many ways, but Casey wasn't up to such a deed.

"Keep walkin', Marsh. We're almost there."

Through a doorway into another building, down a stairway, no easy task for Polansky, and then down another, and still another, down into the bowels of the barraque.

Demon Pawn was the first to leave.

Green could hardly care less. So what if their jobs were gone? His wasn't. They had their following down here in the barraque and they'd fight their way back topside. No one could stop them. Brooky and the others might hold down jobs as well as trying to play music but you couldn't really do it that way. You had to devote yourself. But Brooky didn't want to hear that, not never, and especially not tonight.

So Red was happy to see Kip come in. Usually The Oyster was a great place but Casey George had put a damper on everyone.

"What is this, a wake?" Kip asked.

"It's Casey George's doing," Red told him.

"He's here?"

"Nah, he's gone, spreading cheer through the barraque."

"Glad to hear it. I can do without that sumbitch tonight."

"Where's Flyte?" Kip asked.

"Playing with his new toy."

"I thought you and him was gonna practice."

"You know Flyte. Give him something with lectrical runnin' through it and he goes into pleasure shock."

Brooky leaned over Kip's back. "You're sittin' in my chair, pretty boy."

"You got your name on it?"

"I'm gonna carve my name on it, just as soon's I finish carvin' it on your ass."

Kip turned but Brooky had nothing in his hands.

"Hah! Got ya! Little pretty boy got scared I was gonna carve up his pretty little pretty boy face."

"Lay off him, will ya?" Morrisdaughter said.

"Why should I? Pretty boy here and his friends have bummed it up for all of us. We were workin' on a gig topside but now it's all cinders thanks to these guys."

"I didn't see you tryin' to break up no fights last night. You seemed to be enjoyin' it just as much as anyone. More," Kip said.

"Hey, I got nothin' against a good fight. Especially with the spiffies. I'll take on any five of them any day of the week," Brooky replied.

"Then what's your gripe?"

"No gripe. I just want these squirrels to know that they didn't just screw it up for themselves. They got no class."

"We wouldn't be here if we did," Kip said. Red had already ambled away as soon as he saw that Brooky wasn't really looking for a fight and he was putting moves on Libido, who was trying to ease away from him. "Anyway, all we did was do your work for you. If you'd got your gig, you'd have done the same."

Brooky grinned. "Maybe. Maybe not."

"Will you two cut it out?" The Old Man Himself roared. "I'd like to have a little peace here for a change."

Brooky slapped Morrisdaughter on the butt. "Go give The Old Man a little piece, will you, so he'll shut up?" Morrisdaughter slapped his hand but smiled. Brooky slipped into the seat that Red had vacated. "So what's with your lectron boy? What's he up to?"

"What do you care?"

"What do I care? I care a lot. He's the only one of you three who's got anything going for him. There's dozens of us down here like you and Red but that boy's got brains."

"You know what brains are good for, don't you?"

"They're good for lots of things."

"They're good for getting into trouble, that's all. It was Flyte's brains that started the fight last night, so's he could chrome the topside puter."

"Yeah?" Brooky said eagerly. "I told you that guy had brains."

Red Green's meaty hands fell heavily on each of Brooky's shoulders. "I'm the brains in this outfit, boy. It was my idea to start the fight so Flyte could slip into the manager's office and do his little thing."

"The only brains you got, Green, is in your fists."

"Yeah? You think so, smart guy?" Greene pulled Brooky up out of his chair and, still holding him with one hand, shook his fist in Brooky's face.

"Yeah, I think so." A knife was suddenly in Brooky's hand and he waved it in Green's face. Green grinned.

Suddenly the two young men were in the middle of a circle, Morrisdaughter and Libido both fearful and excited by the prospect of a fight, Kip uncertain, ready to jump in but also afraid to. It was The Old Man Himself however who stopped things. Moving faster than seemed possible for a man of his age, he stood between the two, booming out orders for them to stop.

"Get out of my way, old man," Green said and lunged forward. The Old Man Himself seemed to move his foot just a little and Green crashed heavily to the floor. Brooky took this moment to lunge forward and The Old Man Himself brought up his arm and the knife went flying across the room.

"Get that," he said to no one in particular. Morrisdaughter scurried to retrieve the knife. "Now listen to me, you two apes. Nobody is gonna fight nobody in here, you understand? Nobody fights nobody nowhere. We got to stick together, not fight amongst ourselves. You understand that?"

"Ah, shut up, old man." Green got to his feet. He and Brooky glared at each other but the fight had obviously gone out of them for the time being.

"Give me that." The Old Man Himself held out his hand and Morrisdaughter put Brooky's knife in it. With hands and muscles hardened by fifty years of factory work, The Old Man Himself snapped the blade in half.

"Hey!" Brooky said.

"You can get another one."

Poley touched the back of his head; it was sticky and matted with blood. A scrawny cat raced away at the movement and stopped to watch warily from the shadows before melting away into the night. Poley probed until he found the cut. It wasn't too bad but there was a lump growing underneath it that would be painful for many days. He slowly got to his feet, wincing. There was no one around. That was pure luck. If anyone had found him while he was still lying there unconscious . . . he didn't care to follow that thought to any of its logical conclusions.

He walked steadily to the bar where Skarys was working. No one watching him could guess the pain he was feeling or the effort it took to make him look unaffected by the wound. The bouncer greeted him as he approached but let out a low oath when Poley turned around. "Lord! What happened to you?"

"What does it look like?"

"It looks like somebody axed you."

"You're absolutely brilliant. You ought to be in college. Can you clean this out for me?"

"Just a sec. I'll be right back."

It didn't take long for the bouncer to return with a wet bar rag with which he began cleaning out the wound. It stung.

"What is that?" Poley asked.

"Vodka. Lord, you're going to have a real egg there. Better put some ice on it. I'll get you some in a minute. Who did this to you?"

"I don't know yet. But I'll find out."

"I never thought I'd live to see the day when someone could sneak up on you and axe you."

"It was all Walston's fault. He made me rush things."

"There. That ought to hold you for a while." Poley turned around to face Skarys, who was grinning broadly. "So now you're angry at your protector and benefactor."

"I've always trusted you sooner than I'd ever trust him. You know that."

"Are you going to tell me what happened?"

"I was following someone . . . "

"Marshall Polansky."

"You should be a professor, not a student. Anyway, Walston held me up and so I was rushing to catch up with Polansky before I lost him and . . . "

"You got careless."

"I had no choice."

"Poley, I never thought you'd disappoint me like this. Well, now you know the price of carelessness. By the Lord, give you another ten years and you might become human again. Go inside and ask Tan to give you some ice."

Bluebird got up fifteen minutes before Lady Madonna and surprised her by having breakfast nearly ready when The Lady awoke.

At first Lady Madonna was irritated to find Bluebird preparing breakfast without her help but she quickly stifled her irritation. This was indeed one of the steps that she had been hoping for and, although The Lady was aware that Bluebird had her own ulterior motives for taking it, it was something to be welcomed and encouraged.

"It's remarkable what a good night's sleep will do for one's soul," she said as she entered the kitchen.

"Yes, Lady."

"A good night's sleep, away from the raucous music and riots topside, can almost change one's personality."

Bluebird turned her back to The Lady. "If you're going to make fun of me, you can make your own breakfast."

"I wasn't making fun of you, child."

"I'm not a child and you were mocking. There have been plenty of nights I've spent here and didn't go topside, plenty more than the times I did."

"Of course, girl."

"And I'm not a girl either!"

Bluebird's outburst took Lady Madonna by surprise and she felt anger rising inside her but she managed to suppress it as she realized that Bluebird had a point: although she was a child still in some ways, in many more she was now a grown woman and, like a parent, Lady Madonna had been blind to her growth.

"I apologize, Bluebird. You're right. I did not mean to mock you. I had no right to do that."

Bluebird turned back to her cooking with a muffled grunt.

"Would you like some help?"

"No! I can do it myself! I'm perfectly capable of doing it myself!"

"All right, all right. I was just asking, that's all. Is it okay if I set the table?"

"Yes."

Lady Madonna managed to stifle a chuckle but she couldn't help but smile. Tomorrow she would be making her own breakfast again and probably Bluebird's too but nonetheless a step had been taken and the girl, the child, was truly closer to being a woman.

"Lady?" Her tone had changed.

"Yes?"

"Do you believe in svana?"

"Of course."

"I mean, really believe?"

"What are you getting at . . . Bluebird?" She had almost said "child" and she was sure that Bluebird had heard the hesitation.

"I mean, well, you're not like the other people in the barraque and . . . "

"Of course I'm like the other people in the barraque. I'm one of them and so are you."

"No. They're more . . . superstitious."

"And you think that svana is just a superstition?"

"Isn't it?"

"No. Oh, yes, there are superstitions involved with it. But there's more to it, much more."

"I don't understand."

"It brings us all together, child." Neither Lady Madonna nor Bluebird noticed that she had used the forbidden word again. "For one night, the barraque is one. Svana keeps us together. It reminds us. " She smiled at Bluebird. "It's more than just a chance for certain people to show off their voices."

Daylight had long been streaming into the abandoned factory before any one of the three huddled forms moved. Kip sat up and looked at his companions. Yesterday seemed like some crazy dream, yet he knew that Flyte's rig was waiting for them two rooms away. He longed to put it on again and dive into that warm sea of data.

He realized that it had been a long time since he had eaten. He rummaged around in Red Green's pack but there was nothing there

He turned to see Flyte looking at him. "Did it really happen?" Kip asked softly.

Flyte nodded slowly. "Yeah." He looked at Red, snoring

softly about half a meter away. "It happened."

"I can't believe it but I want to do it again."

Flyte looked at Red again. "Later." He got up and walked to the next room and Kip followed him. Flyte walked to the opposite wall and stood there, looking at the room where the device lay innocently on the floor.

"What is that thing, anyway?" Kip asked.

"It's . . . it's like nothing I ever heard of before, Kip. It . . . hooks you in directly to the computer, so that you experience it directly."

"How does it work?"

"The way I figure it is that by concentrating on particular data, your mind can interpret it in a way that's familiar to you."

Kip shook his head. "You figured all that out?"

"I didn't figure nothing out. It's just a guess. Maybe it's some kind of circuit in the rig that interprets stuff for you but I doubt it."

"Maybe Marshall Polansky can tell us something about it. Someone's gonna be looking for it. They're gonna want it bad. I think we ought to get rid of it."

"We can't, Kip. This thing could be our mealticket."

"I think it's more likely to be our ticket to The Tower." He stopped. Red Green was standing in the doorway.

There was a long, long pause then Red said, "The Tower, huh?"

"We were just talking, Red," Flyte said.

"I heard you. Get rid of it."

"But Red . . . "

"Get rid of it!" he snapped. "I don't care how you do it but I don't want anything to do with that thing."

"Red, you don't understand."

"I understand one thing. People who go to The Tower don't come back."

"Sure they do."

"They're not the same people and you know it. They're different. They even look and smell different. They destroy people there and rebuild them into little flesh robots."

"Don't tell me you're afraid of The Tower, Red."

"Damn straight I'm afraid of it. I'll handle anybody with fists or a knife but I ain't messin' with that place. There's some things nobody can handle. Yeah, I'm afraid."

Flyte stared into Green's unflinching eyes for a long moment then looked away. "All right. I'll get rid of it."

"Good. I'm going to get something to eat. Any of you pussies want to come along?"

Flyte looked at Kip and gave him a small nod.

"Sure, Red. I'll go with you," Kip said. "Flyte?"

"No. I've got to get rid of this thing, remember?"

"You can drop it in one of the reclaimer bins."

"I want to check out a few more things on it then I'll get rid of it. Bring me back something to eat, will you?"

"Sure."

Green stopped in the doorway. "Make sure you get rid of that thing, pussy. If you don't . . . " He left the threat unspoken.

"You're not serious, are you?" Kip asked as he and Red walked toward the fence that surrounded the old warehouse.

"Damn straight I'm serious. Are you on his side too?"

"I'm not on anybody's side. I'm just trying to figure things out. I mean, Flyte says he thinks he can get us unbarred from topside."

"Great. We can perform inside The Tower. Our own captive audience." Red stopped to flip the switch Flyte had installed at the fence. "Kip, you know I'd like to go back topside. But The Tower? No way I'm going to chance that."

They crawled under the fence and Kip flipped the switch at the other side.

"Yeah. That's scary, all right." What was Flyte doing right now? Kip wanted to be with him, diving back into the city puter. No matter how dangerous it might be, it was heady and exciting, a feeling of secret power that was intoxicating. Who knew what they might find?

Casey George felt grimy. A day's growth of beard scratched his hand whenever he rubbed his chin. His clothes were rumpled and felt dirtier than they probably were. His eyes burned and felt caked with sleep-grime; he had only had catnaps during the night. The basement they were in was hot and smelled like old detergent. Polansky slept beside him, the drug that Poley had slapped on him slowly wearing off. He had supported the old man through the maze of tunnels under the barraque until he had reached this basement. It was unlikely they had been followed; he had left Polansky several times and back-tracked, using side tunnels and switchbacks to come up behind anyone or anything that might have followed them. He had seen and heard nothing. He gladly would have left Polansky behind but he dared not. It wouldn't take much to drag enough information out of the old man to threaten them all, even though Polansky knew less than any of them.

He hoped that The Old Man Himself had gotten the message to Demon Pawn but there was nothing else he could do. For all he knew, Pawn was already in the Tower when Poley had tried to waylay Polansky.

He heard a sound above him, so faint that ordinarily he would never have heard it above the other sounds that filtered down to him from the barraque. His senses now, though, were those of a hunted animal and he was on his feet immediately, knife in hand. He moved silently to the cluttered stairway and crouched beneath it. Soon he felt rather than heard someone coming down, stopping briefly at each missing step as if the intruder knew each one by heart. Enough light filtered into the basement that the objects on the stairway could be seen if not defined, but shadows covered some of the missing steps so an intruder who was not familiar with the building could easily miss one and fall. It was no accident that these missing steps were in shadowed places nor was it an accident that the first two shadows contained perfectly strong steps to lull the unwary into confidence.

The intruder reached the bottom of the steps. Surely he could hear the blood coursing in Casey George's veins! Slowly the man moved across the basement until he could be seen and Casey relaxed. "Pawn," he said in a low whisper. The little men turned around. "Were you followed?"

"I don't think so." Pawn looked at Marshall. "Is he all right? What happened?"

"He came into ChiLil's last night, all hot and bothered over things Poley had said to him."

"Poley? That means trouble."

"Wait till you hear. I told Marsh to get out and lie low. I watched and, sure enough, Poley was tagging him. Marsh was moving fast and Poley had to hurry to keep up with him, so I was able to follow them easily without being detected. But I couldn't catch up until he'd hit Marsh with a trank patch."

"What'd you do?"

"I conked Poley and dragged Marsh here."

"Were you followed?"

"I'm sure one of their damn bird eyes watched the whole thing but I went under at Trent's and they haven't come down here yet."

"They will eventually. And eventually won't be very long. We've got to keep moving."

"Moving? Moving where?"

"Don't worry. We'll get out of this yet. But we don't have much time. We've got to get the Ultimate Warehouse. So let's get moving."

It was early afternoon when Poley opened his eyes to stare at the cracks in his ceiling. It was a pleasure not waking up to Walston's whining voice. Poley reached up and touched the back of his head. A scab was starting to form and it was very tender. The knot was larger. There was nothing more he could do about it however.

He already had a good idea who had axed him the night before but he wanted to hear it from Walston himself so at last he got up and punched Walston's number.

"Mister Secretary Walston is not available at the moment," the computer said. "However he wishes to speak to you immediately so please remain where you are and he will contact you in a few minutes." The screen went blank and Poley swore. Then he realized that Walston was pulling the same trick on him that Poley had pulled on Walston the day before, and he grinned.

But he dared not leave—he needed to speak with Walston. True to his word, Walston called back in a few minutes.

"I need your help," Walston said.

"And I need yours. Who axed me last night?"

"What do you mean?"

"Don't try to play dumb with me, Walston. I know a couple of your flying spies were watching us last night. Who waylaid me and where did he and Polansky go?"

"Poley, I've told you before . . . "

"Look, Walston, I don't have time to play games and neither do you. You didn't even bother to pretend you weren't observing me last night."

"I don't know what you mean."

"Are you screaming at me, wanting to know where Marshall Polansky is? Have you been calling me all night? No, you wait until I call you. That means you know what happened. Look, Walston, I want that guy and you want him too. So level with me. Tell me what happened last night. Give me the knowledge I want and I can get you the knowledge you need."

Walston was quiet a moment. "All right, all right. But I want that man, Poley. I want him and Polansky and anyone else who has anything to do with them."

Poley grinned, ignoring the pain it caused. "So do I, Walston. So do I."

There were eyes that saw Bluebird as she descended into the nethermost fringes of the barraque, where The Point melted into Westmeat, where many of the buildings had rusted sheet metal in their windows, eyes that would report to The Lady. Let them. She had her own life to lead and not The Lady's. She passed the stairway that she had taken down from the Zone with so many others only thirty-six hours earlier. It seemed more like thirty-six days. The smell of the river was stronger here and the noise level higher but the people here didn't seem to mind—they were probably used to it. They seemed no different from the people at her end of the barraque, as well-fed, dressed the same except for a gang of young men whose clothes were as loud and flashy as their voices. They paid no attention to her—she was just a mouse, nowhere near as attractive as The Lady had been at Bluebird's age. The only thing distinctive about Bluebird was her voice.

She was lost; following Casey George the night before, she had failed to pay attention to places she could have used as markers. Window signs were almost as infrequent as road signs. She saw people enter buildings that apparently were bars or other establishments with no indication on the outside of what they might be. She was afraid to ask anyone, to let anyone that she was lost and an outsider, and thus possible prey. She had lost her street ways in the years she had been with The Lady; she was no longer a street urchin and she had not learned the street ways of an older girl.

Poley was surprised to see Lady Madonna's girl wandering around as if she were lost. He hesitated a moment then decided that anything that might get him in The Lady's good graces was probably a good idea. He approached her and tipped his hat. "Excuse me, miss, are you lost? Can I help you?"

"No, I'm fine. I . . . " She stopped and Poley waited for her to make up her mind. "I'm looking for a place . . . a bar." It wasn't what he had expected. He raised his eyebrows but said nothing. "The Oyster. Do you know it?"

The Oyster? Hmmm. That's where Red Green and his group hung out. He might be able to find a way to get something out of this after all.

"You're not far from it. Come. I'll show you." He started down the street but stopped when Bluebird did not follow. "You don't have to be afraid. I won't lead you down any dark alleys." Bluebird apparently decided to follow him. "Although, frankly, miss, you might be safer in some dark alley than in The Oyster. May I ask why you wish to go there?"

"I don't see that it's any of your business."

"Of course not. But I might be able to help you. Are you looking for someone perhaps?"

"Perhaps."

"Ah, I see. It is an affair of the heart."

"No. It's nothing like that!"

Her immediate response told Poley what he needed to know but he had to keep her thinking he hadn't understood. "Perhaps a business transaction then?"

"Perhaps."

"Ah." He said no more until they came to a building in the middle of a block that seemed no different from any other except for the sandwich board on the sidewalk alongside. Barely visible large letters on both sides of the sign read simply "The Oyster." The door was open and he could see people inside and hear their voices. He started to enter.

"This is it. Are you coming in or not? Shall I tell someone you're here?"

"No," she said abruptly. "Not right now. I'll come back later."

"Suit yourself. Now you know where it is."

Poley could think of nothing else to do so he went inside and sat down at the front bar, watching through the grimy window as she stood on the sidewalk then walked to Jimmy's Foodbar nearby.

"You want something, Poley?" the barmaid asked.

"You seen Casey George?"

"Nope."

"What about the people he hangs around with?"

"Like who?"

"Oh . . . like Marshall Polansky, for example."

"Never seen him with Polansky."

"You haven't?"

"Nope."

"I see."

The tender moved down to serve someone else. Poley looked around. The Lady's girl had not followed him in. It was probably best to leave well enough alone. He had helped her; surely she would remember him if there came a time when he needed her help.

He finished his drink and left. His next stop would be Trent's Warehouse but the trail would be cold.

"Okay. Where is it?"

Flyte Error looked innocently at Red. "I got rid of it, like you told me to."

"Sure you did. I know you better than you know yourself, pussy. Where you got it hid?"

Flyte motioned toward his box of parts. "Right there."

Red sifted through the box with his hands. "What're you talkin' about?"

"I took it apart. All the parts are there. You didn't really think I'd just throw it away, did you?"

"No." Red ran his fingers through his hair and scratched his scalp. "I never thought of something like this."

Kip grinned. "That's Flyte for you. He's got real brains."

"I don't trust you, pussy. You liked that thing too much to

take it apart."

"I didn't say I couldn't put it together again if I wanted to. I got the knowledge up here." Flyte tapped the side of his head with a finger.

"Yeah, but you got nothing down here." Red cupped his crotch and grinned.

"I'll match you inch for inch any day of the week," Flyte retorted.

"Hey, it ain't size that counts, it's how you use it."

"Yeah, that's what all you little guys say."

"Listen, you little runt . . . "

Kip grabbed Red's arm as he started to move toward Flyte. "Cut it out, Red. You asked for it. We got better things to do than fight each other."

"Like what?"

"We gotta get us another gig, for one thing."

"I can live without one."

"Don't you like standing up there in front of the tufts, making them think you're something hot?"

"Sure. But I can live without it."

"What about it, Flyte? You done anything about getting us another job?"

"Ah, why bother with that little pussy? You know they ain't gonna let us topside for a long time."

"I put out a notice after you guys left this morning. Let's see if anybody's answered it yet." Flyte's fingers moved across the keyboard.

Kip peered over his shoulder. "Look at that, will you, Red? We ain't been banned after all."

Red joined him. "Sheeet! News travels fast, don't it? We is in demand. Everybody wants us. There must be half the joints in the Zone who's interested in us."

"Look at that. Cannibal Soup will pay us twice what the Money Marriage did."

"Didn't," Flyte said. "We never got a nixie from them."

"The hell we didn't," Red said.

"Well, only the credit I chromed from them."

"Which was more than they was gonna pay us in the first place."

"Cannibal Soup," Kip said. "That's Fleet Street. We do them and we got wings."

"Yeah, if Red don't fuck it up."

"I'll be a good boy, Flyte." Red patted Flyte's head. "Tell 'em yes and let's set a time."

Things were not going well at all. This was not what Benj Walston was used to. He was accustomed to everything going smoothly with only a few minor glitches here and there. But the control web was gone, probably forever. He had perused the list of what else had been stolen that night and the rest of it was mostly prototypes that were easily replaceable. Nothing else worthwhile had been stolen.

The web had been in his lab only because it had recently been delivered and had not yet been assigned to a research lab for further development. But now it was gone, gone forever. Walston was certain of that. He had to go through the motions of trying to find it but he was certain that that would be futile. It had already long been spirited out of the city, probably even before they had discovered it was gone. However, there was always the possibility that it was still somewhere in the city, probably in the barraque, while they waited for the tumult to die down.

And then again . . . there was always the possibility that they didn't know what they had. In which case, it was best not to tip his hand. It might still be somewhere in the barraque, if it had not already been picked apart and destroyed in an attempt to find out what it was.

Walston was used to dealing with multiple possibilities and difficult choices but the pressure of this one was more than he preferred. If only Poley would come up with something.

Unfortunately Poley now had a score to settle with Casey George and he might do something foolish instead of reporting his findings to Walston.

"What are we going to do?" Marshall Polansky, the tranks finally out of his system, had woken up. "How are we going to live?"

"Lord, Marsh, will you shut up?" Casey George was getting annoyed at Polansky's whining.

"We're marked men. They'll be looking for us everywhere. I never should have agreed to do this."

"We're prepared for this," Pawn said. "We've got hiding places everywhere in the barraque. They'll never find us."

"We can't keep moving every night," Casey said. "Eventually they'll find traces of where we've been. We've got to find some place safe and stay there indefinitely."

"I'll never see my children and grandchildren again."

"You know, Marsh, I'd turn you over to The Tower personally if I could do it without putting myself in danger."

"You would?"

"I would. Now shut up and stop whining! If you can't do anything to help, then just keep quiet while Pawn and I figure this out."

"We don't have to worry about being found out, Casey. The squids don't have eyes or ears down here. We might be discovered by 'quistes but not by this 'they' you're so worried about."

"I'm not so sure. Walston and his crowd are pretty sneaky. And don't forget Poley and people like him. They may be 'quistes but they're not with us."

"We can take care of Poley."

"Sure. He's got a bone to pick with me after last night. He's going to want to pay me back."

"He doesn't even know who hit him."

"Want to bet? I was out on the open street too long for those damn flying spies not to identify me. Hell, they were probably following Marsh and Poley all along."

"You think so?" Marshall asked fearfully.

"Lord, Marsh, you think those guys are up on top because they're dumb? If they were as smart as you, we'd all be living their lives and they'd be down here."

"I tried, Casey. I did what you told me."

"No problem, Marsh," Pawn said. "You did good. You did just what you were supposed to. Once Poley was on to us, we didn't have any choice."

"Okay. What do we do now?" Casey asked.

"We go even deeper. Tonight we move to the old Ultimate Warehouse. It goes deeper than any other building in the barraque. Its lowest levels go below the depth of the riverbed."

"Is that supposed to make me feel safe?"

"You'll be as safe there as you would in your own bed."

"That's what I was afraid of."

The comm winked on and called for Lady Madonna's attention. It was the tender at The Oyster who apparently had turned on the phone remotely with a warning for Lady Madonna not to answer vocally.

"Who you lookin' for, hon?" It was the tender.

Before Lady Madonna could ask her what she meant, she heard Bluebird say, "I . . . I'm looking for someone."

"Aren't we all? Who you lookin' for, hon?"

"I . . . I don't know his name. I saw him up at the Money Marriage the other night and I know he comes here sometimes . . . and I . . . "

"You must mean Red Green. Hon, take my advice and stay away from him. He's nothing but bad news. He tried to start a fight here last night."

"No, not him. He's the singer, isn't he?"

"If you call that singing."

"I'm looking for the autar player."

"Kip Marten. Now, he's a sweetheart. The three of them, you know, they been blood for a long time."

"Blood?"

"Brothers, buddies, family, whatever you wanna call it."

"Is he here? I mean . . . "

"Nah. It's too early in the day for them to be comin' in here. None of them gets up before the sun clocks out. You want me to be tellin' him you was here?"

The tender tried to get her name but Bluebird refused and finally blurted out "I . . . I'll come back later."

"Did you get that, Lady? What should I do?"

Lady Madonna told her to do nothing unless Lady Madonna called back, thanked her, and turned off the comm. So Bluebird had gone down to the warehouse section of the barraque. She probably thought she could get away with it, that The Lady would never find out. Or perhaps she didn't care. The girl had a mind of her own and often contradicted The Lady's wishes even when she knew she would get caught. Well, she had never wanted to break the girl's spirit and it looked as if she never would. But there were too many currents in the stream now and Bluebird was out where she might not be able to get back to shore if things got too rough. Lady Madonna considered going down to The Oyster and bringing her home but decided against it—there would be time to do that later if the situation warranted it. Her eyes were everywhere in the barraque, seeing and hearing things that the mechanical spies of the city's police would never know. It had been several weeks since The Lady had been outside. She was becoming too dependent on Bluebird, becoming like so many topsiders, staying in their rooms and never leaving, all their needs and necessities brought to them, slaves to their HVs and the master computer. She frowned. She had not meant to become like the enemy, though it was not the city people who were her enemies. Her real enemies were bigger: the ennui of everyone, top and bottom alike, and their failure to deal with the inequities and dissatisfactions of the system.

She would go out again. Tonight. But not yet. She had to stay home and wait for her eyes and ears to tell her what was happening.

They wound their way through the maze of tunnels under the barraque. Casey George had thought he knew them well but he was soon lost and confused. It seemed as if no one had come this way for years. Even Demon Pawn stopped several times to convince himself that they were going in the right direction. There were few working lights and the walls were damp, often covered with slimy growths. Casey was surprised that it didn't smell too bad, just musty and damp. Rats watched them fearlessly from the shadows, wondering perhaps what these creatures might be, maybe the first they had ever seen bigger than themselves.

"Are you sure you know where you're going?" Casey asked when Pawn stopped for the third time.

Pawn just held up his hand to silence him. After a moment, he started forward again.

"Well?" Casey said.

"I think I know where I'm going."

"You think?"

"I'm pretty sure. It's been years since I've been down here."

"It looks like it's been years since anyone's been down here."

"It might be."

"I thought I'd memorized those maps they gave us but everything's all different and twisted when you're down here. It's not just lines on a couple of pieces of paper."

"Who do you think made those maps, Casey?"

"Huh? I don't know."

"I made them. There was a time when I knew this place like the back of . . . no, better than the back of my hand. It's strange."

"Sort of like coming home, huh?"

"I never thought I could ever forget what it was like down here. But I was wrong. It's funny how easily you can forget something that once was so important to you."

"Well, you better not have forgotten too much."

"Don't worry. I'll get us to safety."

"There's no place that's safe. No place." Marshall had been so quiet that they had forgotten about him. Never the noisiest of people at any time, he had almost become a ghost down here.

"Just shut up," Casey snapped.

"It's all right, Marsh," Pawn said softly. "I know what I'm doing. I knew where we're going."

"We'll never be safe," Marsh repeated. "I'll never see my children again, my grandchildren." A solitary tear ran down his cheek. Casey turned away from him, angry yet also stricken with remorse. Marsh was paying the highest price of the three of them.

Now they sat in a small damp room underneath the Ultimate Warehouse. It was easy to believe they were below the depth of the river bed. The entire floor, a honeycomb of small rooms like the one they were in, was cool and damp, with moisture on every wall. Some of the rooms were essentially empty but many of them were full of rotting boxes and rusting machinery. In one, the remnants of an old vehicle, tatters of fabric still hanging from the rusted frame, caught Casey's attention for some reason. There was a not-unpleasant musty smell in the air. Pawn had searched through several of the rooms until he had found the one he wanted. There, wrapped in rodent-proof plastic hidden behind old rotting boxes and crates, enough food and supplies had been stored to keep them alive indefinitely. But who in their right mind would want to stay down here indefinitely? Marshall was right: they would never be safe.

Pawn found what he had been looking for and plugged a lamp into a wall socket. To Casey's surprise, the lamp lit immediately and chased the shadows of the room far away, to lurk behind the crates and boxes to lie in wait outside the doorway.

"What is this place anyway?" he asked.

"I told you. It's the sub-sub-basement of the Ultimate Warehouse, the deepest place in the barraque."

"How can you be sure?"

"Believe me, it is. We've checked every single building in the barraque. Nothing else even comes close."

Casey grunted. "What about these rooms? What were they used for?"

"Storage mostly, I guess. I think a couple of them were tool bins."

Casey walked over and shined Pawn's flash into one of the disintegrating crates. It was nothing but a mass of old paper, forgotten magazines and print, fused together by the dampness, covered with mold and slowly rotting away.

The sudden surge of current flashed through Flyte Error's mind like a lightning bolt, cutting a jagged painful path and leaving behind a brief afterimage. It was so close it took him only picoseconds to track it down and, when he did, adrenalin surged through his physical body, making the picoseconds slow down even further subjectively. Someone had just plugged into a socket only four floors below him! It had to be the squids or some other government agency, working their way up towards him, ready to bring him to justice at The Tower. Who else could it be? It was only a power outlet and so he could not find out who or what had just plugged into the electrical system but the current flow indicated it was probably only a single lamp. Of course. They would need light and they would not want to indicate to him who they were.

He started to cut himself out of the circuit but stopped—there was no place to run, no place to hide, where they would not be able to find him. His only hope lay within the circuit, within the puter. It was their eyes, their ears, their mouth, their master, and he was part of it now, a living conscious essence inside a mute mindless brain, and here he would have to hide and fight them.

Here was where all the secrets were hidden, all the information and knowledge that he needed to control his pursuers. All the answers were there and so, of course, all the dangers as well.

Poley didn't like it, not one bit. He hadn't bothered to try to find out from Walston which entrance Casey George had taken into the warehouse. It didn't matter. All the entrances were sealed up tight except for two. But no matter which entrance he had taken, Casey George would have gone down to the basement and the tunnels, and that unnerved Poley. He should have asked Skarys to come with him. Poley knew the alleys and the empty buildings well; he knew his way into a few that seemed impenetrable to everyone else. But the tunnels were another matter: they honeycombed the ground underneath the barraque and they were dangerous places. One could get lost there easily. Even without getting lost, one could slip in the slime and lie there unconscious or unable to move for days.

His flash lit only a short distance ahead, glistening off the wet walls, catching the moving shadows and glinting eyes of rats whose claws scrambled and scratched constantly around him in a threatening sibilance while they squeaked to each other as if making direful plots against his body.

It was hopeless. He would never find Casey George down here. He could have gone in any of a dozen different directions. Patience, patience. He would wait. It would not be the first time. He had not survived by jumping precipitously into things. Casey George could not stay underground forever. Sooner or late, he had to surface and, when he did, Poley would be waiting for him.

Benj Walston's main room was filled with everyone on the Council, just as each of their main rooms was likewise filled. It was the first time they had all met at once in more years than Walston could remember. There had always been at least one and usually more missing for various reasons whenever they had met recently—some because of more pressing business, some because of illness, some because they probably just didn't feel like getting out of bed that morning, certainly not for the boring details of keeping the city running. That was Benj Walston's job. But this was to be no ordinary run-of-the-mill meeting.

"How could you allow this thing to happen?" The speaker was the oldest of the members, the patriarch of the Mont'Illiano family, who ran the communication industry. Parchment skin, nothing left of his long nose but a paperlike beak, thin bloodless lips, eyes rheumy but still shrewd, he had, despite his age, been the most faithful of the Council, not ready yet to let go of the reins of the control, although all of his sons had already died and his grandson, nearly as old as Walston, stood by his side, more than ready to take control when his grandfather finally faltered. "Where was this so-called force of yours? Where were your spies?"

"There is no such thing as complete security, Damien. You know that."

"Benj, you have failed us. You have failed us completely."

The other members of the Council watched them, the unspoken truce between the two that once had seemed so unbreakable now seemingly about to break into a battle that might prove worse than the loss of the piloting device. Yet it was exciting, more exciting than anything their HVs could bring them.

"I promised you nothing, Damien, nothing but to do my best, which I have done. If it's not enough, perhaps you know someone who could do better."

95

"Perhaps I do, but the damage is already done and it's your job to correct it and bring us back to where we should be."

"The lab director is working on it."

Mont'Illiano snorted. "Pinder? He's competent enough in his field but he doesn't have the necessaries to create something like this."

"No. But much of the knowledge is already in the computer banks and every expert in the country is examining it. It should not take long to recreate it."

"And how much would that cost us?"

"You had no idea this was about to happen?" one of the others asked.

Of course I knew, Walston felt like saying, *but I just thought it would be fun to chase ghosts around the city and make you old bastards sweat,* but instead he snapped, "Of course I didn't know. Don't you think I'd have taken steps to prevent it if I'd known they were planning something like this?"

"The puter," another said. "Have you searched the puter for information? Surely it's all there."

"Even the computer's resources are limited," Walston said patiently. "It can't overhear every conversation in every room and on every corner in the city, much less those in the barraque."

"What about your vast network of spies?" Mont'Illiano asked in a sarcastic tone of voice.

"There are only a handful in the barraque, not nearly enough to keep tabs on all those who rate our suspicions and, to be quite honest with you, I don't fully trust any of them. Furthermore, it doesn't take long for the 'quistes to figure out that they're working for me and then they're useless. Worse than that, in fact, because the 'quistes feed them false information."

"Then why bother?" Mont'Illiano asked.

"Because false information is meant to lead us away from the truth, so I merely have to place the computer on that path and frequently we find exactly what it is they're trying to keep us from knowing." Walston did not think it wise to let Mont'Illiano know of the times when misinformation was not the opposite of some important knowledge but rather just the playful misleading of his informants by some barraquiste who enjoyed tweaking their noses.

"Get that device back, Walston," Mont'Illiano said sharply. "I don't care what it costs you." His image winked out.

Walston looked around him at the other members of the Council, who all seemed to be nervously fidgeting. "If there's no other business, then the meeting is adjourned."

Bird was on her way and there was still plenty of light. She was safe and so it was safe for The Lady to venture out into the streets herself. The girl could easily find her way back to where she belonged. Where she belonged! The Lady smiled. Once she had belonged to the streets. Did she really belong here, with The Lady? That was her own decision and The Lady couldn't force it.

She stepped out into the street, nodding hello to those who passed by, stopping a moment for idle chatter, as if she hadn't a care in the world as she moved steadily toward the square.

It was dangerous but it had to be done. Pawn slipped out of the Ultimate Warehouse and approached the small building next to it. He had never been there before but he had memorized everything that had been sent to him. He went to the riverside door and punched in the key he had been given. The door opened to an innocent-looking office with a comm but no vid. Pawn punched in some numbers. He heard a click at the other end as someone picked up the comm but no one said anything.

"This is Wings," he said. "We're in the big raft and we need help."

The voice at the other end was electronically altered.

"We'll jump you out tomorrow. Watch for visuals this evening on the other side. You know the codes?"

"Yes."

"We may have to flood as a diversion. You know the sequence?"

"Yes."

"Good. Watch the other side near seven."

"But how will you get us out?"

"The Lord will see to everything. Do you understand?"

Pawn smiled as widely as he was sure his contact was smiling. "Yes. I understand."

Smoke rose from the campfires of squatters. A couple of them fought over a rusting cast iron cog. A few people trudged aimlessly along the pitted roads where trucks rumbled slowly. One of the people seemed to be moving less aimlessly than the others, moving inexorably toward the warehouse while still seeming to move randomly from one side of the road to the other. From his perch above the crowd, Pawn could see that he was coming steadily toward the warehouse. Then he recognized the gait, the build of his body, his clothes. As Pawn watched, Poley stopped in a secluded corner and clamped something to the guard wires and the building's gate opened for him.

"What do you want?" Walston snapped when Poley called. "Have you located Polansky and Casey George yet?"

"They're under the barraque."

"Brilliant. I want to know *where* under the barraque they are."

"Do you know what a honeycomb of basements and tunnels and conduits are down there?"

"I don't want excuses. I want results."

"I'm not going down there. That's flat."

"Do I detect some fear in your bold and intrepid character?"

"I'm not crazy, Walston. There's nothing to be gained by wandering around under the barraque in hopes of finding Casey George. It would be very easy to get lost down there and there are many other places I'd rather be lost in."

"So what do you suggest?"

"We've got to flush them out."

Walston started to laugh uncontrollably while Poley looked at him in puzzlement until Walston finally regained control and dabbed at his eyes.

"Can you let me in on the joke, Mister Secretary?" Poley asked. "I don't see what's so funny."

"Nothing, nothing." Walston giggled a little bit more. "It was just the thought of them being flushed out of their tunnels, I mean, really flushed . . . " Walston stopped.

Poley caught on almost immediately. "Can it be done?" he asked.

"I don't know. Computer!"

"Yes, Mister Secretary?"

"There are gates, aren't there, sluices, something, I don't know what they're called, but some way of routing river water into the basements of the barraque?"

"It might be possible, Mister Secretary. Originally the basements were sealed off from seepage so it would have been impossible years ago."

"But is it possible now?"

"I am searching the records, Mister Secretary. They're quite old and access isn't as readily available as current data. Some are even offline and will have to be loaded. It won't take long."

"Are you saying you don't know? Are you telling me, computer, that there are things you don't know?"

"There are many things I don't know, Mister Secretary. But I can route the river water through sewage pipes and tunnels, if you wish."

"That wouldn't help."

"Many of the gates have not been used for over a century

and have been used as passageways from one building to another, so it is quite possible, probable even, that most of the basements are now connected to each other even if they originally were not."

"Are you telling me . . . ?"

"Yes, Mister Secretary. It would appear that over ninety percent of the buildings in the barraque are now interconnected and they could be flooded by river water. But it would not be advisable."

"Why not?"

"The structural integrity of the buildings would be compromised."

"What the hell is it talking about?" Poley asked.

"So if I ordered you to open a gate that would flood the basements . . . "

"It would not be executed."

"I see." Walston leaned his elbows on his desk and put his chin on his folded hands. "Let us both see a map of the gates. It might be possible to flood only selected areas of the barraque."

Walston was suddenly in the middle of a 3-D map of the basements of the barraque.

"Blue highlights the gates that are under my control, which originally allowed water into selected factories. But the breached basement walls and interconnections make it unlikely that flooding could be contained within a small area."

"Are there any manual overrides?"

Poley watched carefully, trying to comprehend what Walston was leaving unstated.

"Only this one." The main gate became a brighter blue. There were still three side gates that would let in lesser amounts of water. Poley looked away from his screen a moment, then back, nodded his head slowly, and smiled.

"Are there any gates that can only be operated manually?"

Two more gates appeared on the map. "Their condition is unknown. They may no longer be operational. They were last used, according to my records, one hundred three years ago."

"Poley. Check those out when you get a chance. Do you know where they are?"

Rust would be a serious factor but, over that span of time, it might act in their favor. "I've got everything memorized, Mister Secretary. I have all the knowledge I need."

"Thank you, computer. That will be all for now." The two manual gates suddenly went red. "What was that?" There was no answer from the computer. "Computer! What happened? Why did those gates go red?"

"Offline loading. Stand by. Additional information coming in." Walston scowled and Poley was puzzled. He had never heard the computer speak in fragments before. "Manual gates no longer operational. Sealed fifty-three years ago to prevent breakthroughs due to deterioration." The three computer-controlled gates that could also be manually controlled went red. "All manually controlled gates have been similarly sealed."

"Why didn't you tell me this in the first place?" Walston yelled.

"This information was not online. It had been archived and it had to be located and loaded manually. Such operations are time-dependent, Mister Secretary."

"If you don't need me for anything else, Mister Secretary, I need to check on some things."

Walston looked straight at Poley. The smile was gone and his expression was as grim and angry as he supposed his own was. "Go ahead," he said. "Check out everything you can."

"I will." Poley smiled tightly and broke the connection.

As they walked through Westmeat toward The Oyster, Red babbled on about how great it would be if they could perform at Cannibal Soup. It was all Kip could do to keep from laughing out loud at him. No, he didn't need to perform at all. Not much he didn't.

And then he saw her. Kip could've sworn it was the same

girl he had met so briefly at the Money Marriage, turning the corner as he and Red approached The Oyster.

Red was already inside The Oyster's doorway before he realized that Kip hadn't followed him and was staring at something down the street. "Hey! What's the matter with you?"

"Nothing. I just . . . I just remembered. I got to see someone."

"You got to see someone? Who the hell you got to see?"

"No one you know."

"Bullshit! I know everyone you known and lots more besides. You just getting' light in the head like Flyte."

"I'll be right back." It was all Kip could do to keep from running after the girl. He turned the corner and there she was, a full block ahead of him and going straight. She was probably heading for the main street out of Westmeat. But what could he do? He couldn't just go up behind her and grab her shoulder and say, "Hi. Remember me?" Well, maybe he could. She did seem to like him. But he wasn't sure and he couldn't afford to take the chance. He hated to lose sight of her again but he couldn't see that he had any choice.

He dodged down an alley. Now he could run without her turning around to see him. He tripped over some trash, knocking debris over with a clatter, sprawling and scraping his elbows and knees, only to pick himself up immediately—he had to get in front of her somehow, make it all seem an accidental meeting. His breath came in great gulps; he simply wasn't used to this. It had been a long time since he and Red had raced away from the squids. Even the other night, their exit from the Money Marriage had been more of a joyous romp, taken leisurely, surrounded by other 'quistes.

He stopped just before he got back to the main street, brushed down his clothes, swept his hair back with his hands, and stepped out of the alley just as the girl was turning the corner. He started toward her. What could he say that wouldn't sound stupid? Would she even recognize him? Of course she would. She had seen him onstage at the Money Marriage all night, hadn't she? Still . . .

She looked at him and he couldn't miss the sign of recognition, the little jolt as she stopped in her tracks and her mouth fell open just a little bit. Kip grinned. "Hi. We meet again."

She smiled back at him.

Demon Pawn was gone. "I have to check some things out," he had said, leaving Casey with Polansky, who just sat in a corner, mumbling to himself, helpless, useless, worse than useless. Why in the world had they ever recruited him? The Polish Avenger, indeed! And now Casey had put himself into Demon Pawn's hands. It did not make him feel comfortable; it did not make him feel comfortable at all.

And what the hell were they supposed to do to pass the time? There was little enough to talk about. There was no HV. There was nothing to do but think. Polansky was right; in a few days, they would all be stark raving crazy.

"Casey. Come out here."

There might be a truckload of squids out in the rotting corridor with Pawn but Casey didn't care. He had to get away from Polansky, who never even looked up at the little man's whispery voice.

"What are you being so hush-hush about?" Casey growled as he left the storeroom. "Who the hell's going to hear us? Or how the hell are we going to keep them from hearing us if they already can?"

"There are devices that can detect very faint vibrations far underground."

"Maybe they'll think we're an earthquake. What do you want? Where did you go?"

"I needed to explore a little and refresh my memory. Also, I had to talk to someone."

"Will you quit being so damned mysterious?"

"You want to get out of here?"

"I'd love to. And Walston and Poley would also love me to get out of here too. So I think I'll stay. Take Marshall. He's already so far gone it doesn't matter."

"We'll have to leave the city but it's already arranged. Tomorrow."

"You're crazy. All we have to do is walk out on the street and those flying spies of Walston's will have us nailed."

Even in the dim light of their flashes, Casey could see Pawn's grin. "Those things operate on infrared. And in a little over twenty-four hours, their sensors are gonna be overloaded."

"What are you talking about?"

"Svana."

A young man several years older than Kip, his face already gray and lined, shambled past them, muttering, "Smoke, smoke."

Dozens of dreams and fantasies and still Kip did not know what to do. Show this girl around the barraque? Hadn't she lived here all her life, just like him? What was there to show her in The Point that was worth seeing? The three-story building where he and Red and Flyte had first performed? It was abandoned now, falling in upon itself, full of tepid, foul pools of standing water, rats and vermin, and the remnants of countless furtive assignations left behind to rot and decay.

The smell of the river was stronger here and the noise level higher but the people living here didn't seem to care; they seemed no different from anyone else in the barraque, except for a gang of young men who paid no attention to Bluebird and Kip.

This section of the barraque was a maze, streets blocked for no apparent reason, temporary ramshackle buildings erected at the end of a block, piles of trash in the alleys, their smell mixing with that of the river. Rotting roofs showed fire-blackened beams. Archways were festooned with laundry on lines. Trucks careened down the pitted roads, rattling loudly as they swerved and swayed at corners. Peddlers loudly proclaimed the quality of their wares to women in embroidered dresses while old men and some not-so-old men mumbled in doorways, sometimes reaching out a hand to a passerby. Children played in dirt and women gossiped in the squares.

"There's really not much to see down here," he said at last.

"There's really not much to see anywhere," she replied.

Kip lifted the meager strands of wire by a faded No Trespassing sign and they walked past an abandoned warehouse or factory with rusted metal rollback doors. Crumbling mortar surrounded an odd-shaped stone at its base. They walked out on a decaying pier; buildings around them cast greasy shadows on the oily water.

There was music in the wind that whistled like a wand over the river. Waves made by a passing rivercleaner crashed against the walls that protected the buildings' basements, where debris gathered and bobbed in the water. They sounded like the simulated cymbals of Flyte's keyboards. The calls of the everpresent seagulls were like single notes falling from Kip's autar and the grinding of the rivercleaners was like Red Green's gyrations in front of an audience.

"Oh, Lord, is that a baby?"

Startled, he looked toward where Bluebird was pointing, then laughed. "No. It's just a doll. See?" The tide had turned it so that now an empty socket was revealed where once there had been an arm.

"I thought it was real," she said in a shaky voice.

They sat down on the edge of the wharf and looked across the water to the recycling plant on the other side, which sprawled across the bank and stained the river from its many outlets. Further upriver they could see the bridge with its constant freight of truck traffic, so high above the barraque it might have been on another world. A shift of the fetid breeze brought with it the stench of excrement.

"Do you come here often?"

"Come here often?" Kip laughed. "I live here."

"No. I mean, to this pier."

"Oh. No, not often. Not anymore. We used to come here when were just little kids, me and Red and Flyte."

"Uh-huh." She was looking at him as if there was nothing else in her world.

"I mean, it was tighter then. The fence was solid and you had to crawl under it down there, where the shore falls away. One mistake and you could wind up in the river."

"Did you?"

"Me? No, I never did. I came close a couple of times but Red always saved me at the last moment. Red went in a couple of times and Flyte . . . well, he's smart but he's not always the most graceful thing around, you know? He went in a lot."

She laughed.

"What about you? What's your name?"

She hesitated a moment. "Bluebird," she said in an almost inaudible voice.

"That's an ay-kay, right?"

"Uh-huh." She looked away from him but not before he saw the look on her face.

"Hey, look, I'm not meaning to pry, okay? Just . . . you know, some people have strange names."

"Like Red Green?"

"Hey, that's real, you know. I mean, the Green is his. And the Red part, well, you know, just look at him."

"Sure. I understand."

A gull flapped by close to them then turned away.

"Kip Marten's for real too. Flyte, he's the only one of us who's gone for ay-kays so far. I don't know why. Red, he don't really care, I guess. Or maybe he's proud. Or he likes being called Red Green, I guess."

"And you?"

"Too much trouble. I'm Kip, I've always been Kip, and I

don't see any reason to change."

"I got reasons. Lots of reasons. I've changed so much in the past year. I don't feel like Bluebird any more."

"Hey, that's okay." He picked up a tiny piece of cement that had flaked off the pier and tossed it into the river.

"How does Canary sound to you?"

"You like birds, huh? Why not Sparrow?" He tossed another piece of cement at one of the birds.

"Sparrows don't sing."

"Are you trying to tell me you're a singer?" Kip tried to remain calm but now he thought that maybe she wasn't really interested in him but was just trying to get into a band.

"That's what's been happening to me for the last year. I've been learning how to sing."

"So you used to be a bluebird and now you're a canary, is that it? I've never heard either of them sing."

"Neither have I."

He looked out at the river. "I heard a meadowlark once. It was in a Stefan Coldrider episode. He was in one of the wilderness areas."

"I've never been there. I've never been out of the barraque."

"Me neither. I've heard there's a zoo uptop but I've never seen it." Maybe he and Flyte could check it out. Then he remembered that the device was probably going to be scrap soon, if Red Green had his way. "The only wild animals I've ever seen are sparrows and rats and pigeons."

"And seagulls." She looked out over the river wistfully. "They're so free. I'd like to go to the wilderness areas and be free like that."

"They say that the wilderness areas aren't really free, that they're managed and controlled, that nothing is free any more." He threw another piece of cement into the river. "If we had a transplat, we could go there."

She shook her head. "I don't think I could ever get into a transplat. I'm afraid I wouldn't be me when I came out the other end."

"Well, it doesn't matter. We don't have one anyway."

Kip couldn't think of anything else to say and apparently neither could she. It was several moments before she said, "Meadowlark. That sounds a lot better than canary. Canaries are caged birds. I don't want to be caged."

"Me neither. But how come you're a better singer now?"

"I told you. I've been learning."

"How do you learn to sing? You either do it or you don't."

"You learn to sing better. I was a good singer a year ago but now I know how to control it, how to come down on a note, how to breathe . . . "

"How to breathe?" Bluebird wasn't making any sense at all.

"Never mind. It took me a year to understand all these things. I can't explain them to you in ten minutes."

"Where did you learn all this stuff?"

"I have a teacher. She . . . " Kip waited as Bluebird paused, apparently not wanting to say anything else. Finally she said, "She heard me during svana . . . "

"You sing at svana?"

"I used to. I didn't sing for the last two. The Lady didn't want me to and . . . "

"Lady? What Lady?"

Bluebird looked down at the wavelets beneath their feet. "Lady Madonna," she said in a small voice.

"You work for Lady Madonna?" Kip felt like he was shouting the words.

"I'm her student, that's all."

"And I'm sitting here like this with you? Why didn't you tell me before?"

Bluebird laid her hand on his arm. "It's all right, Kip. She doesn't own me. I'm just her student."

"She's trouble. Nothing but trouble."

"That's not true! She . . . she . . . "

"She runs the barraque. She's an agent for the city."

"Kip, where did you hear things like that?"

"Everybody knows it. You never heard it?"

"I . . . I did. Before I met her. But it's not true, Kip. I swear it. It's not true."

He looked at her suspiciously. "Did she send you?"

"No. She'd be very upset if she knew I was here."

"Great! That's just what I wanted to hear."

"Kip, please."

A stale breeze from the river ruffled her hair. She was beautiful. He loved her. He was afraid of her.

"How can I trust you?"

"You have to trust me yourself. I can't make you trust me."

Kip got up and held out his hand. "Let's go."

"Kip, please."

"I gotta have time to think. I want to trust you, Bluebird, but I'm afraid to. You don't know what's happening. Lord, even I don't know what's happening right now. There are so many things goin' on, so many changes."

He wanted to go back to the warehouse. Maybe he could find out something through that device of Flyte's that would help him figure things out, some way he could find out whether or not he could trust her.

As they started to leave, Kip saw Poley walking by on the street outside the fence. He started to turn around but it was already too late—Bluebird saw Poley too and waved to him. Poley stopped a moment, waved back, and kept going. Now Kip was really frightened.

"Why did you wave to him?" It was only through an effort that he kept from shouting the words at her.

"He helped me a little while ago. He showed me where The Oyster is."

"The Oyster? Why did you want to go to the Oyster?"

She looked at the ground for a moment, like a little girl digging his toe into the cracked tar of the street. "I heard you and Red and Flyte went there."

Kip looked closely at her. There was no sign of deception on her face but, if she were an agent of the city, she would easily be able to deceive someone like him. "Do you have any idea who that guy is?" The Lord was against him, no doubt of it. Just when he'd finally found the girl, this Bluebird . . . and then to find she was Lady Madonna's girl! It wasn't fair! The knowledge frightened him. And then, when he was about to take her back to the warehouse with him, Poley had to pass by going in the same direction.

"I don't even know his name. I never even saw him before until an hour or so ago. What's the matter, Kip? What's wrong?"

"That's Poley. Stay away from him. He's bad news. He's not someone you want to know. He's not someone anybody wants to know. You'll always wind up paying for it, one way or another."

"What do you mean?"

"He's one of Walston's men."

"Walston?"

"Benj Walston. You know, the guy runs who runs the city and all its squids, the guy who got us kicked out of the Money Marriage the other night."

"I thought that was Red Green's fault."

Kip grinned. "Well, yeah."

"I know who Benj Walston is. But what do you mean when you say that that man is one of Walston's men?"

"He's a spy. He lives in the barraque but he sells us to the boss man, you understand?"

"I'm not sure."

"Never mind. It's too complicated to explain. Just stay away from him."

"He was nice to me."

"Oh, he's always nice," Kip sneered, "right up until the moment he sticks his knife in your back."

They crawled under the wire to the rubble-strewn road that

passed by the old pier. Poley was nowhere to be seen. "Okay. Since you want to see it, let's go to The Oyster." Kip started off in the direction opposite the one Poley had taken.

As The Lady had expected, Gloria was sitting in the square. The sun was still high enough to light occasional patches and Gloria, as usual, was sitting in one. The Lady sat down beside her and waited. It was peaceful. Occasionally another barraquiste would walk through, nodding respectfully to them both but no one spoke to either of them. A window in a building on the other side of the square was cracked, with bulls-eye rays radiating out from the central jagged hole. Most of the vendors had packed up their meager wares, though there was still a handful on the opposite side of the square. A few of the inevitable sparrows came down to pick at invisible crumbs and, in the dark edges of the buildings, rats waited for the night.

A dust devil began at the far end of the square and whirled away for about thirty seconds, picking up dirt and loose paper then dropping them out of apparent boredom, and disappeared behind a sheet metal shack.

"Tomorrow night," Gloria said, as softly as the dust devil had laid down its burdens.

"Tomorrow night. Thank you, Lady."

"I am no Lady," Gloria said. "I would not take that upon myself."

"Whatever you may say, you are the most revered and honored of us all."

Gloria's laugh sounded like pebbles tossed about by the breeze. "Honor. Reverence. What are they worth in the barraque?"

"They are worth what we make them worth. Without them, life would be worth much less."

"And what is life worth in the barraque?"

"It is worth as much here as anywhere else, perhaps

more."

Another dust devil appeared, closer to them this time. "You have your answers down so firmly, don't you, my little one?"

"The answers change, as I learn more. What answers do you have?"

"None. Not any more. Once I thought I knew so much, perhaps even as much as you think you do but now I know better. The only knowledge that time brings is that knowledge is worth nothing. It will not buy you a single bite of chocolate on the market."

"I can set no price on knowledge. It is too dear for any price."

"Oh, my dear, my dear!" The dust devil disappeared again, perhaps frightened away by Gloria's cackle. "The price of your knowledge is just too, too dear."

After waiting an appropriate time for Gloria to calm down, Lady Madonna got up. "Thank you once again, Gloria."

She was ten or more steps away when she heard Gloria say softly, "Knowledge is worth nothing."

So Walston wanted Poley to check out those gates, regardless of what the computer said. It did seem suspicious that the data changed so suddenly, as if someone was tampering with the puter. But that didn't make any sense. Nonetheless he'd check it out, not because Walston wanted him to but because the computer might be wrong. After all, it was only human and Poley wasn't one to trust what others, human or puter, told him: if he could check out his information, he had to check it out. Lack of knowledge was useless but wrong knowledge was worse. That could cost him a lot of time and a lot of trouble.

In any case, although he hated to admit it, even to himself, Poley didn't know what else to do. The idea of literally flushing out Casey George and Marshall Polansky appealed to his sense of humor but he didn't appreciate it when the puter said it could cause the destruction of numerous buildings. Walston didn't care of course. He didn't have to live here.

The nearest gate was inside one of the busiest warehouses still operating, turned into a factory by the work on the starship and full of people day and night. Poley wasn't on particularly good terms with any of them and certainly not with the foremen and bosses, so he headed for the other manual gate, in the first subbasement of the old Ultimate Warehouse. As he passed one of the old piers, he was surprised to see Kip Marten and Lady Madonna's protégé exiting through the old wire fence that daunted no one. Before he could get out of their line of sight, the girl had seen him and waved. Poley waved back and kept walking.

Flyte Error was frightened.

He had seen their faces, heard their voices, unaware that a human being was watching and listening to them through the computer interface.

It had been easy to change those gates to Permanently Inoperative and then let the computer explain what had happened, but it had made Walston suspicious, though he couldn't possibly know that Flyte was manipulating the puter, could he? It didn't matter—Poley was on his way to check out the gates and soon the basements of all the warehouses and factories in the barraque would be flooded and then there would be a collapse that would destroy most of Westmeat. Flyte Error was certain of it, having experienced it in a digital manner that Walston and Poley could not possibly understand.

There was no way that Flyte could stop Poley. He could have kept Walston locked forever in his apartment which he never left anyway, but there was nothing he could do to Poley. Red Green might be able to help him but how could Flyte explain things to Red without letting him know he hadn't really taken the gadget apart? Kip would help him but he was probably already half drunk with Red, and Flyte didn't dare leave the warehouse because that was the logical place where Poley would go, since the other manual gate was in an active factory.

And then there were those people several floors below him. Apparently they weren't agents of the city after all; maybe they could help him. He had to warn them but he knew he'd get lost in those catacombs without the computer to guide him.

He left commands for the computer to override any opening of the manual/computerized gates, not knowing whether or not those commands would have any effect or even if the computer would actually try to follow them, but it was the best he could do. He would have to intercept Poley somehow and keep him away from the gate in the Ultimate Warehouse. Maybe by then Kip and Red would show up and . . . it wouldn't work. He knew it. There was no way it could work. But he had to try.

Unwillingly, he disconnected himself from the computer and re-entered the real world.

"Where's your precious mates?"

Red looked blearily at Brooky. "What?"

"Kip and Flyte. I thought you was blood."

"We are. Been blood all our lives. F'rever."

"Then where are they?"

"I dunno."

Across the table, The Old Man Himself watched. Red wondered if he ever left the Oyster. He was always here when Red arrived; he was still here when Red left. He always had a drink at hand but he was never drunk.

"Sounds like your blood's getting' pretty thin."

Red didn't like the sneer on Brooky's face. He got up and had to grab the back of a chair for balance. He missed it and went sprawling on the floor, feeling the chair stab into his ribcage.

Brooky looked down at him, the sneer still on his face. "I wouldn't fight me, if I were you. You're in no condition to fight anyone. If I were you, I'd go find your blood."

Red grabbed the edge of the table and hauled himself to his feet. He noticed that, despite his words, Brooky stayed out of reach. The Old Man Himself hadn't moved.

"I wouldn't stoop to fightin' slime like you. Gotta go find someone in my own class." He started out, grabbing the sill of the doorway between the back room and the front bar.

"You had enough, Red," the tender said. "I ain't servin' you any more today."

"I don't want none of your swill anyway." He navigated the gantlet of bar stools to the front door, surprised to find the sun still shining. The breeze off the river slapped him in the face as he stepped out into the sunshine. He thought of going around the corner to see if Kip had gone to the Horse but really all he wanted to do was just curl up in a corner somewhere and go to sleep.

Kids were playing Crosse on the pile of rubble in the center of the square, just as he and Kip and Flyte and others had done so long ago. That pile had been there as long as he could remember. He wondered if the kids still called it the Tomb of the Unknown Wino. As he watched, the kid at the top of the pile shoved another one down roughly then fell off as he was hit in the face with a rock. He wished he was a kid again; it had been so simple then.

What had Kip said? He had to see someone. Who the fuck did he have to see? Maybe they were at the Horse. Kip had to see someone about a Horse. He started to laugh and threw up on the sidewalk.

He knelt for a while at the edge of the street, bile streaming out of his mouth. It wasn't the first time and he was oblivious to the people who looked at him with distaste, even the hardline boozers who looked down at him because he couldn't hold his liquor. The kids playing on the rubble weren't interested at all in this red-haired man puking his guts out by the side of the road.

A man. He wasn't even twenty yet but to them he was an old man, no different from their fathers or even their grandfathers. Just the thought made his bones ache. Well, fuck it! Fuck them all! Fuck Kip! Fuck Flyte! Fuck Brooky! Fuck The Old Man Himself! He was going back to the warehouse and he was going to sleep all day and they could all just fuck themselves.

A man who might have been in his mid-thirties reached down with his one good arm to pick Red up. The other arm had been amputated at the elbow, the ragged scars of the stitches showing in pink against the dark stump. "Green, Green, Green," he said. "Don't you never learn?"

"Doily! Where the hell'd you come from?"

"Just passin' through when they threw you out of The Oyster."

"They didn't throw me out. I walked out on my own two feet."

"Stumbled out, you mean. Sometimes I think you never learned a thing from me, Red."

"I try, Doily, I try. But it's hard sometimes."

"Well, you take care now. I ain't gonna be 'round every time you be needin' some help."

"I'm okay. Thanks, man." He started down the street, occasionally stopping to lean against a building to let his head clear. Every time he looked back, Doily was still there, watching him sadly.

Casey George had explored all the rooms in the lowest basement of the old Ultimate Warehouse. One room was a small convenience, stained and smelly; the remains of an old vehicle of some kind rusted away in another. Casey suspected it was fuel-powered rather than electrical-driven. There was little left of it, all the upholstery and soft material decayed and long gone, perhaps eaten by vermin. Only the rusted and corroded metal frame was left and a few other metal parts still attached to the frame.

Casey wondered what it must have been like in the days when this kind of vehicle ruled the roads and people could drive them unencumbered down empty highways from city to city. It would be so easy for them now if they could just get into some such vehicle and drive away to some other metropolis, to start a new life with new ay-kays under a new puter. But it wasn't going to be easy for them. They hadn't told Marsh yet what was going to happen to them but Casey knew he wouldn't want to do it, him and his damned children and grandchildren!

So maybe they'd leave him here, to rot in the cellars of the old Ultimate Warehouse. But Casey knew that he wasn't being fair to the old man. Once he too had been full of dreams and action, just as Casey and Demon Pawn were now, and he had paid for those dreams. They would watch out for him . . . somehow.

Red was not at The Oyster, though most of the rest of the crowd was, of course, The Old Man Himself watching from the far end of the table. Kip wondered if he ever left the Oyster—he was always there when Kip arrived; he was still there when Kip left, always with a drink at hand but never drunk.

Brooky swaggered up to Kip. "You missed your blood. You shoulda seen him—he was out there puking his guts out on the curb."

"Which way did he go?"

"Who knows? Who cares?"

Bluebird and Kip fought their way back through the crowd in the front, Old Toothless John smiling up at Bluebird as if he thought he was some kind of HV star.

"What are you going to do now?" Bluebird asked, apparently unfazed by the customers at The Oyster. "Are you going try to find him?"

"Who knows where he went. Red knows every dive in the

barraque. If he wants something, he knows where to get it."

They passed buildings of fire-blackened brick, barbed wire, and rusted metal drums. He scrambled onto a pile of rubble and helped her up then down into the empty shell of another building.

"But this is against the law."

Kip laughed and she laughed with him. "Everything's against the law. Look, no one cares about these old buildings any more. You know how many people sleep here?"

He was beginning to feel good again. She seemed unfazed by the rats and vermin, the trips through dark hallways and tunnels. Perhaps she was even impressed. It certainly couldn't be anything like the life she led with The Lady, that was for certain. This had to be exciting and romantic to her, living on the edge of existence, where the wine of life was dearest. He let out a holler as they passed the remnants of wood pallets drying in the sun.

"What was that for?"

"Just felt like it."

"It wasn't a signal of some kind?"

"A signal? What for? To who?"

"I don't know. To Red Green, maybe."

"Red ain't hearing much of anything right now, I can tell you that."

Kip went from one building to another, successfully managing to keep them out of the streets as much as possible.

"What about the little guy who plays keyboards?"

"Flyte Error. I don't know where he is. He might be just around the corner or he might be miles away."

"Will he be where you're taking me?"

"Could be. I don't know."

He hoped that Flyte wouldn't be there but it didn't matter. There were plenty of rooms at the warehouse. They had chosen the building for their headquarters because it was so far away from anything else and hard to get into. It was as safe as any place in the barraque could be. Even so, they always made sure to cover their tracks.

They crossed from the second floor of one factory to another on an overhead bridge between the buildings. There was still glass in the windows, mostly jagged shards around the edges of the frames.

"Can't we stop for a while? I'm getting tired."

"Sure. We're almost there anyway." He pointed out the empty window frame. "That's it over there. See?"

"That old building over there? It's big but it's not much. You got it all to yourselves?"

"Pretty much."

The building towered over its neighbors, many of which were little more than piles of rubble. In the vacant lots where buildings had been razed long ago, some barraquistes searched among the remaining partial walls, rusted grillwork and electric outlets sticking out of the cement and concrete, trying to find something that would still be of use to someone else. Other barraquistes huddled around fires that sent wisps of smoke into the stagnant air while others hurried past them on the streets. Feral dogs darted among them, sometimes snapping something up between their legs or out of their hands. Grass and weeds and even an occasional sapling fought their way through the chunks of concrete and brick and rotting wood, nature reaching out to claim her own.

"Look!" Bluebird pointed. "Isn't that the man we saw down by the dock?"

It was Poley all right. A few more seconds and he disappeared behind a building but there was little doubt: he was heading straight for the Ultimate Warehouse.

"Come on!" Kip grabbed Bluebird's hand and started for the nearest stairwell.

"What's your hurry?"

"Flyte's probably in the warehouse all alone and he wouldn't know how to handle Poley if he had a whole troop of squids on his side."

"What is it? What's your hurry?" she cried as he pulled her

down the stairway.

"That's Poley, don't you see?"

"So what? He's not bothering anybody."

Kip stopped in the doorway of the old warehouse. People, many of them wearing rags around their feet and waists, their faces made leather by the relentless elements, wrinkled long before their time, looked at them without curiosity.

"Look." Kip pointed. "He's heading for our warehouse."

"Okay. What about it?"

"That's where me, Red, and Flyte doss out. If Red was there, he could handle ten of Poley for breakfast."

Bluebird giggled then stopped.

"But, Flyte, he's a different matter. And he's probably there right now. I mean, Red and I left him there and he looked like he was going to stay. He's got brains and sometimes I think he's part puter himself but I wouldn't trust him in a fight."

"But isn't he your friend?"

"Right. That's why I'm going after Poley. You can stay here if you want."

Bluebird looked at the people outside. "I'll stay with you."

"Good girl." He put something in her hand. It was a knife.

"But I still don't understand. Wouldn't Flyte do the same for you?"

They moved out into the street; Poley was nowhere in sight. He looked at her, puzzled, but didn't stop moving. "Sure."

"Then why wouldn't you trust him in a fight?"

"Oh." Kip's laugh was brief. "He'd try to help me, all right, but he wouldn't be very good at it. He'd probably get beaten to a pulp long before Red or I would."

"Oh."

"But don't get me wrong. Flyte's worth his weight in diamonds. You remember that fight at the Money Marriage the other night?"

"Of course. I was there, remember?"

"Right." Kip then proceeded to tell her how Red had started the fight so Flyte could chrome the puter and get them some extra credit. "And that's not all. Somehow . . . " He stopped, realizing he was about to tell her something that was just between him and Flyte.

But she wouldn't let him get away. "Yeah? Somehow what?"

"He, uh, somehow he tapped into the puter so we're no longer banned from the Zone and now Fleet Street wants us at twice what the Money Marriage was going to pay us."

"That's great!"

"So we're on our way to the top. Me and Red and Flyte, we're a team like no other. With Flyte's brains and the way Red gets people excited, hey, nothing's gonna stop us now."

"Don't forget yourself."

He felt his face grow warm. "Ah, I'm just a musician."

"You're a great musician. One of the best." She clasped his arm in both of her hands and pressed herself against him.

"Not yet. But I will be. Someday I'll be the greatest autar player there ever was."

"I believe it."

Kip stopped and started to come out of his cloud. "Hey, this ain't the time to talk about stuff like this. We gotta go help Flyte. Come on."

Poley was nowhere in sight when they reached the warehouse.The old signs on the forbidding fence that surrounded it were still legible: NO ADMITTANCE. EMPLOYEES ONLY.

"Are you sure this is where he was going?"

"I don't know where else he coulda been going. Anyway, we can't take the chance. Come on."

Kip reached under the burned-out and gutted shell of a forklift then crawled under some rubble and appeared on the other side of the fence. "Come on. The bottom wire's not live. Flyte took care of that long ago."

She hesitated a moment then followed, flinching when her

back came in contact with the wire. Her clothes were now just as dirty as his.

He reached back under the rubble. "Now it's live again. Flyte did that for us," he said proudly.

She looked up at the building and its gaping windows looked back emptily at them.

Benj Walston stared at the screens that showed him a quiet, controlled city and a quiet but seething barraque. The cameras mounted in the city high over the barraque told him nothing. There had been a time when he had been young and strong, when he had strode the streets of the city and the barraque, when he had owned them in a way that Casey George and that weasel Poley would never know. He was getting old and jaded. He no longer had the daring that had brought him to this position in the first place. In the old days, he wouldn't have hesitated to send several squadrons of police into the barraque to do what had to be done. Now he relied on an unreliable weasel.

Bluebird had not returned by the time Lady Madonna came home. She should have been back by now but of course there were many other places she could have gone. There was no reason for her to come straight back here. After all, The Lady didn't own her. Still she couldn't help worrying, as if Bluebird was her own daughter, the child she and Tor Rosedahl had never had, had never really had the opportunity to bring into the world.

"No, she hasn't come back here," the tender at The Oyster said. "But I'll check."

The Lady made a few other calls. In a few minutes, nearly every street in the barraque would be watched by someone in the net and it wouldn't be long before Bluebird was spotted.

What could that girl be doing with Kip Marley? The thought kept beating through Poley's brain as he headed toward the Ultimate Warehouse. At first he had thought it was bad luck that he had run into her like that but then he realized that it didn't matter. She didn't know where he was going and neither did Marley. Nor were they likely to care. It was another bit of knowledge that he might be able to use some day. Exactly how wasn't clear at the moment but it was something he could hold over the girl to get something from Lady Madonna. Not many people were in that position, though he was also aware that it could easily backfire on him. You didn't play around with The Lady without getting burned. But it was nice to know he had something he could use if he found himself in a corner.

But there was no immediate use for it. The important thing right now was to find out if the gate inside the Ultimate Warehouse was operational or not. If it wasn't, then he would have to check those that were also controllable by the puter. If it was, then there was something weird going on inside the puter.

It would be nice if he could keep such information from Walston until Poley had a use for it but Walston would want a report. Besides, Poley wanted to see Casey George flushed out of those basements as soon as possible.

Gone again! Leaving him trapped down here with Polansky. Pawn. No, it was Casey himself who was the pawn. He had thought he was in control of the unit, leading the raid, picking up the instructions, but all along Demon Pawn had been watching over his shoulder and subtly guiding him. He could see it now. Who do you think drew up those maps? All along, he had known twice as much as Casey but had let him think he was the leader.

Casey felt angry and betrayed, even though a little part of him deep down told him that this was the way it had to be, that this was the way movements were run, wheels within wheels within wheels, until no one, not Demon Pawn and surely not Casey George, could see the whole scheme.

Yet up there, up at the top of the chain, someone pulled the strings, someone saw everything clear and lucid, like a scientist looking down on a maze instead of the poor creatures trapped inside, able to see only one wall at a time. He had always assumed that that someone was a barraquiste like him but now it occurred to him that the movement might be run by a topsider, for reasons other than those that had brought Casey to it, for reasons which might not please Casey if he knew what they were.

Pawn was gone, to get details of how to escape from this damp chilly prison. It shouldn't be that difficult for Casey to find his own way out. All he had to do was find a stairway and go up. Polansky wouldn't even know he was gone.

She should never have gone out. If she had stayed at home, then Bluebird would not be lost now. But that was foolish thinking—Bluebird would have done whatever she wanted to do whether or not Lady Madonna had stayed home. But where could she have gone? She seemed to have disappeared utterly from the barraque.

The thought brought The Lady up short. Was it possible? She quickly brought up recent arrest files. Nothing. That didn't mean a great deal. She wormed her way into the Tower's records. There had been no new entries today.

She hit the clear button but instead of returning a blank screen, the computer returned a view of the barraque from the city. It took a long moment for her to realize she was looking at the old Ultimate Warehouse. The scene seemed to be scrolling backwards. When the scrolling stopped, the camera zoomed in on one of the people who had been walking backwards. The

Lady recognized Poley. She waited but nothing more happened. She asked the computer to scroll forward and watched as Poley moved behind a bulding. She caught one more sight of him and then he was gone. The view changed to another camera, another glimpse of Poley, and then nothing much of interest.

But why was this happening? She was being told something, but what? And by whom? Apparently Poley was going to the Ultimate Warehouse or somewhere nearby. That meant nothing to her. She would have to search. She put her hands to the keyboard and stopped, as Bluebird suddenly appeared on the screen on the same street where Poley had been, a young man beside her.

"Stop!" The screen froze but Bird was already hidden behind a building. "Scroll back." Bird and her friend stepped backwards until they were framed by a gap between two buildings. "Stop. Zoom, center. Down a little. Stop."

Bird was in the middle of the screen, with that damned musician with whom she was so enamoured. What was his name? Marlin. Something like that. What was she doing with him down in Westmeat?

Bluebird had gone too far. She couldn't just sit idly by; she had to do something. But she kept staring at the screen, at Bluebird's frozen face, finding it hard to think.

"Get me Nick Skarys," she said at last. It was time to call in one of her chits, one that she had hoped she would never have to use.

Flyte Error sat on the floor of the vault, feeling woozy and sick. His stomach rumbled; he realized he'd had very little to eat in the last twenty-four hours. He had been too wrapped up in this insidious device. Even now he wanted to put it back on and dive back into those breaking waves of data.

What could he do to prevent Poley from opening those

flood gates two floors below him? Not only would it drown the poor souls in the bottom subbasement but it would also destroy his home, The Ultimate Warehouse, and probably quite a few other buildings in Westmeat as well.

He cracked the door of the vault. After all these years, it still moved silently as he opened it and slid out. He waited, listening, hearing nothing but muted sounds from outside. He was alone in this part of the building.

He moved toward the stairwell, stopped, felt in his pocket. Yes, he still had his flash.

He hesitated in front of that utter darkness then plunged in, his flash pitiful and weak against the powerful blackness of the basement. Slowly, carefully, he inched his way down two flights of cement stairs, occasionally glimpsing signs of rust in the periphery of his flash. The air was close and musty, dry green-brown growths everywhere. The only sounds were the faint rustle of rodents and the loud beating of his own heart.

The route to the gate was etched in his brain but it wouldn't have been difficult anyway to find the room where it was placed, centered in the third subbasement, taking up much more than half of that floor. An old generator, slowly rusting away, dominated a quarter of that space, and smaller machines were scattered about the floor between the stanchions and broken heavy brackets where other machines had once been attached. The river wall was dominated by the floodgate, with half a dozen or more wheels placed about to control it. What in the world could they have thought of, to place that agent of destruction in the bowels of the warehouse? What possible good could it do?

Flyte knew from his communion with the puter that it was not a simple gate—there was an outside gate, an inside gate, and still one more in between them. Working them properly took coordination and understanding of how they were meant to operate. It occurred to Flyte Error that he was probably the only person in the city or the barraque who knew how to work them properly. That didn't mean that Poley couldn't wreak havoc in his ignorance, though he'd probably destroy himself in the process.

Flyte ran his hand over one of the wheels and flakes of rust showered to the floor. He didn't know what do. He didn't know when Poley would arrive or, really, if he would come at all. He started back to the stairwell when he heard someone coming down, two floors above him, while, at the same time, he heard someone else coming up the stairwell at the other end of the building. Flyte looked around in panic for a few seconds then hid behind the huge generator.

Poley moved swiftly into the warehouse, staying close to the outbuildings until he had entered. The silence unnerved him and he jumped when a sparrow suddenly flew out. But there was no sound from any of Kip Marley's crew.

He had no trouble finding a stairway—as he had expected, there was one at the end of the building, not far from where he had entered. There was probably another one at the other end and one in the middle. Any elevators would be useless now.

Poley went as quietly as possible but silence was impossible on the stairway, with its accumulated litter. He would have liked to descend without the use of his flash but he dared not—there was too much debris on the stairs.

Poley saw signs of recent passage, which could have been made anywhere from ten minutes ago to over a week. They had probably been made by one of the kids. There were fewer signs of traffic after the first flight, as if only one other person had gone down further in the recent past. The footsteps in the dust looked very recent indeed. Whoever it was, they had made no attempt to hide the fact that they had been there. Poley could find no indication that anyone had gone back up the same stairway.

The footsteps stopped on the same floor where the floodgate was located and headed toward the center of the building. Whoever it was might have gone back up another stairway but Poley became even more careful.

Demon Pawn stood in the shadows near the landing just above the entry closest to where he had last seen Poley. It seemed to take forever before he heard him moving carefully down the stairs. Pawn took out his knife and waited. Poley was going down, which meant that Poley knew that Casey was in the basement and was going down to get him. But what Poley didn't know was that Pawn would be right behind him.

He moved down the stairway and stopped at the head of the next stairway down. He could see the faint glow of Poley's flash. He followed him slowly, holding his breath whenever Poley stopped for more than a few seconds, wondering if Poley was about to turn around and come back up. He would be in no position to conceal himself if that occurred.

But Poley kept going down, slowly but inexorably, one flight, two flights, three. Then he stopped and went into one of the side rooms. Pawn hesitated on the landing above. If he went down and Poley returned, then Pawn would be discovered. But if Poley went to the other side of the building and took the other stairway, all would be lost. It would be just like Poley to be that devious.

Pawn moved down the stairway one slow step at a time, staying close to the wall. He had nearly reached the bottom of that flight when he saw the faint glow of Poley's flash.

Pawn inched the last few steps and peered around the corner of the doorframe but his caution was not rewarded—the glow was coming from the room beyond the immediate one. Carefully Pawn entered and looked into the next room.

The room was cavernous, covering well over more than half of the entire floor. Poley was shining his flash over a monstrous metal doorway set in the riverside wall. Pawn wondered for a moment what Poley was up to, then he realized that the doorway was the rivergate to which he had been given the operating instructions. He had thought he was probably the only person in the barraque who knew how to operate it but now he began to wonder if Poley also knew.

The warehouse was definitely not a pleasant place. They had to step carefully to avoid slimy patches where old chemicals oozed out of rusting containers. The walls were stained with pigeon droppings and other unidentifiable stains. Bluebird jumped as a pigeon suddenly flew in then back out, probably as startled as she was.

"The place is full of those damn things," Kip whispered. He held his hand up for silence then motioned her forward. She followed him up a stairwell, making more noise than he thought wise, although he wasn't all that quiet himself. He led her to a large empty room, cleared of most of its rubble. "This is where we usually sleep," he said.

"Where is everybody?"

"I don't know." He sat down on a small pile of concrete blocks. "I thought Flyte would be here. Maybe . . . maybe he went to The Oyster. Maybe he's okay."

"I need to rest." She sat down next to him, laying her head against him.

"Sure." His voice was soft and he reached out and put his arm around her.

"Kip," she said softly, "I've got to get back pretty soon. The Lady will be missing me. She probably already has her spies out looking for me."

Kip felt a chill creep over him. "What does she do, follow you everywhere you go?"

"No." She squeezed his hand. "It's not like that."

"What's it like then?"

"Well, she just worries about me, that's all, and she knows so many people, so she just kind of keeps tabs on me, that's all."

"You know what it sounds like to me? It sounds like prison. That's what it sounds like to me." Kip shifted position and she had to raise her head from his shoulder.

"No, it's . . . well, yes, sometimes it seems like prison to me too."

"Right. That's why I left my mother and that's why you should leave her. It's not right."

"She keeps tabs on the whole barraque too. I'm just a small part of . . . "

"And that's not right either!"

"Keep your voice down, Kip. I thought you said . . . "

"Why should we have Mama Madonna looking over our shoulders all the time? It's bad enough that they keep us down here all the time and won't let us upstairs unless we wipe our asses and leave all our snot down here. Why should she be poking into our lives too? She's got no right, you know that. She's got no Lorddamned right!"

"Quiet, Kip. You're shouting. I thought you were afraid of Poley."

"He's not here. He went somewhere else. I just got worked up over nothing."

"You got worked up, all right."

"Hoy, Kip, Flyte! What're you guys shouting about?"

"It's Red." Kip stood up. "Lord knows what made him come back here before dark. I'm up here!" he shouted. "I don't know where Flyte is."

"Kip, let's get out of here before it gets dark, okay? Please?"

Kip put his arm around her protectively. "Sure." He turned to face her. "Look, I'm not trying to, you know, just put moves on you. I mean, I am, but . . . but that's not all. I want to see you again. I want to see you a lot and I don't want to scare you off, so if I come on too strong, you just . . . "

She kissed him briefly on the lips. "You're sweet, Kip."

"Well, isn't this a lovely sight?" Red Green said.

There was a horrendous squealing like a giant sheet of metal was being torn in two by some machine gone berserk and Kip felt as if the whole building had moved.

Casey George went up a few steps at a time, shining his flash to check his progress then turning it off unless there was something in the way that might cause him trouble. So he was able to see the glow from someone else's flash in a room two levels above the level where they were camped. It was probably Demon Pawn but Casey hadn't survived in the barraque or in the movement by assuming something was true until he had checked it out.

He moved slowly into the room next to the one where the glow was coming from, slowly putting each foot down one step at a time until he was sure of his footing, until at last he was able to peer around the corner of the doorframe to see Poley puzzling over the controls of a large door that took up most of the riverside wall.

It didn't take long for Casey George to realize what it was.

Poley hadn't counted on being underground and possibly trapped when he opened the floodgates and let the waters roll. There had to be some kind of remote control. He shined his flash around the room but saw nothing that looked remotely useful. There was an old cast iron furnace, so huge it must have been put in place before the building had been completely built. There were a couple of other pieces of heavy equipment whose purpose wasn't plain to him but there was nothing in the immediate vicinity of the gate.

There had to be some way to open this damn thing safely.

Poley looked at the control wheel closest to him. He set his flash on the floor and grabbed the rim of the wheel. Large flakes of rust showered to the floor and bit into his palm. He put both of his hands on it and tried to move it but it was rusted shut. Or . . . he tried turning it in the other direction with similar result. Putting all his strength behind it, he tried yanking it a couple of

times in each direction. He thought he felt something give in
the clockwise direction. He definitely felt something give in his
back. His muscles weren't used to this kind of exertion.

He jerked it a couple more times in the clockwise direction
then put everything he had into turning it in that direction.

Something gave.

There was an enormous shudder that felt as if it had moved
the entire building, and a shrieking of tortured metal that deafened
Poley and made him fall to his knees, his hands up to his ears in
a futile attempt to protect his eardrums.

Though the noise ended almost immediately, Poley felt
as if he was enfolded in cotton and he was completely taken
by surprise when someone bowled into him and knocked him
rudely to the hard cement floor.

"You can't do that!" The words were far away and muffled.
He looked up at his attacker, dimly visible in the diffuse light of
his torch, which had also been knocked over, and recognized this
young man but could not place him. He was thinking too slowly.
But, without his even thinking of it, his foot had reached out
and upended his attacker, who fell heavily to the concrete and
howled in pain. Poley was immediately on top of him, pressing
his knife to the young man's throat.

"What do you think you're doing?"

"You can't . . . you can't . . . " Every gasped word made the
point of Poley's knife stick into the soft flesh under the young
man's jaw.

Poley pulled the knife back a centimeter. "I can't what?"

"Can't . . . can't open that gate. It'll . . . it'll destroy all of
Westmeat."

"How do you know?"

"The puter . . . projections . . . the physics . . . equations
. . . "

Poley pressed he point of the knife back against the young
man's flesh. "How did you know about this? What were you
doing here? Were you waiting for me?"

The young man looked at Poley with terror. "N . . . n . . .

n . . . no."

"I don't believe you."

It had all taken Pawn completely by surprise. First Poley had yanked on the control with all his might and nothing had happened. It had looked as if his efforts were going to be in vain. Then there had been that overwhelming sound of metal scraping against metal, screeching and complaining about being roused from their sleep of a hundred years and or more.

And then that kid had come racing out of the shadows to attack Poley. He was, of course, no match for Walston's's wily agent and now it looked as if Poley, thinking that he had no witnesses, would kill him.

He was about to move out to prevent it when he saw someone else move on the other side of the room . . . Casey George was stealing out of the shadows and slowly moving in on Poley, who was too intent on Flyte Error to even think that someone else might be anywhere near him.

Pawn smiled and waited for Casey to get far enough into the room that Poley wouldn't see Pawn moving in behind him just as quietly while the young musician babbled and cried.

"What the fuck was that?"

Red Green wasn't the most eloquent person in the world or even in the barraque but Kip Marten agreed whole-heartedly with the question.

"Let's get the hell out of here!" Kip grabbed Bluebird's hand and started for the doorway.

"What about our stuff?" Red yelled.

"To hell with our stuff!"

"I ain't leaving without it." Red stuffed his meager belongings into his shoulder bag and tossed Kip's autar to him.

"Here. You might want this some day."

"Come on, Red, will you? The whole building might be about to fall down around our ears."

"What about Flyte's stuff?"

"You gonna carry it?"

Red grinned. "Yeah. I got my stuff. Fuck Flyte. Let's drift."

They raced down the stairs although everything was quiet now and the building once again seemed as solid and stable as the earth itself. They reached the ground level and started for the outside when Red grabbed Kip's arm. "Wait! I think I heard something."

"Red, if everything's all right, we can come back later."

"Shut up!" Red raised his hand as if he were about to strike Kip and Kip obeyed. For a moment, he heard nothing then he heard voices coming up from the stairwell.

"Lord, they must be trying to blow up this old building." Kip started toward the exit again but Red headed for the stairway. "Where the are hell you going?" Kip demanded.

"Ain't you got ears, Kip? Flyte's down there. We gotta go help him."

"But . . . the building . . . " Kip looked around fearfully, as if he expected the building to collapse around them at any moment.

"Don't you understand, Kip? Flyte's blood. He's blood." Red pulled a flash out of his shoulder bag and started running down the stairway.

"Here. Take this and get the hell out of here." Kip handed Bluebird his autar and took off after Red, barely worrying about the litter on the stairway, stumbling over it, kicking it aside, scraping his palms on the rusty old railing whenever he had to grab it to regain his balance.

Someone else was yelling. The voice was familiar but he didn't have time to worry over who it was. The important thing was that Flyte was in trouble. That was all that mattered to Red Green. Flyte, Kip, and he were blood, thicker than blood, in fact, and he couldn't run out on him, no matter what Kip or Flyte himself might do if it had been Red who was in trouble. And so Kip had to stay with Red, no matter what might happen.

"What's going on down here?" Red demanded as they came down into a large sub-basement.

Kip saw Flyte Error on the floor while Casey George, Demon Pawn, and Poley were all facing each other. Casey George and Demon Pawn both turned at the roar of Red Green's voice and Poley took that moment to attack Pawn, who turned just in time to see Poley coming at him. He slashed at the agent with his own knife but Poley just knocked him over and kept going, right into the arms of Red Green.

"Come on, Red," Poley said. "Let me go. We're on the same side, aren't we?"

"He was gonna knife me, Red." Flyte Error was on his feet again.

Green grabbed Poley's wrist and twisted his arm viciously, grinning with pleasure. For all his skill and experience, the little man was no match for Green's weight and muscle, and the knife clattered to the floor. Green grabbed Poley's other wrist and held both of his hands behind his back. "Someone want to tell me what's going on down here?"

"He was gonna flood the barraque," Flyte Error said. "He was gonna open the floodgate here."

"No such thing," Poley said. "You think I'm crazy?"

Someone touched Kip and he turned around to see Bluebird. "I thought I told you to get out of here."

"Here." She tried to slip his knife back to him.

"Keep it. I got another."

Red was grinning. He was having the time of his life and all Kip wanted to do was get out of here—this old building was seeing more people today than it had probably seen in decades.

"You, crazy?" Red said to Poley. "You see more clearly than any of us. You see round corners." Red pushed Poley before him, toward Flyte Error.

"Look, Red, I got no fight with you. Even now. Let me

explain things."

"You was gonna knife Flyte."

"No, I wasn't."

"He had his knife against my throat, Red. He wasn't kidding."

"Hey, look, you know, a guy thinks he's all alone down here and suddenly this kid comes out of nowhere and knocks me over. I got a bit jumpy. You would too."

"What were you doing down here?"

"I told you, Red. He was gonna flood the . . . "

"Shut up!" Red flung Poley down at the base of the floodgate. "Stay there! No funny business." He looked at Casey George and Demon Pawn. "You two. Stand over there." He pointed to a spot against the wall a meter or two away from Poley.

Casey looked at Pawn, who nodded, and they both obeyed—Pawn seemed to be amused and Kip could see that that pissed off Red.

"Take off your shoes!" Poley started to protest but Red roared the command again and Poley obeyed and tossed them aside. "Now your shirt."

"Really. This is . . . "

"I don't trust you, Poley! Take off your goddamned shirt!" In a few minutes, Poley was completely naked, his clothes in a pile a short distance away.

Green told Kip to go through the clothes. He found two more small knives and two devices that neither of them recognized, as well as some patches and pills.

"Put 'em all over there." Red motioned to the far wall.

Even though he was now at a disadvantage, Poley seemed unconcerned. "Can I put my clothes back on now?"

"Go ahead."

Poley put his shorts on and began to put on his trousers.

"Wait a minute. That's all for now."

Poley smiled held his hands up, palms open, dropping the trousers to the ground. He looked over at Kip Marten. "What're you doing with Lady Madonna's girl?" he asked.

"What?" Red's glanced flickered toward Bluebird briefly. "Is that true?"

"I wouldn't say I'm her girl."

"Is it true?" Red roared.

"I'm her protégé." Bluebird's back seemed to stiffen. "I'm not her girl."

"What the fuck does a protégé do?"

"She's teaching me to . . . "

"Never mind. It's not important right now. What's important right now is what we're going to do with Poley." Red glanced at Casey George and Demon Pawn. "And maybe you guys too."

"He was trying to . . . "

"It's just a . . . "

"We don't know anything more than . . . "

"Shut up!" Green roared as they all tried to talk at once. "Poley. You're first and it better be good. No one'll ever find you down here."

"You talk tough, Green, and I wouldn't want to face you in a knife fight. But I don't think you could kill a man in cold blood."

Red grinned. "Wanta find out?"

"Look, you know I work for Walston. That's no secret. But I work both sides of the street. You know that too. I was down here checking out something for Walston and I saw this thing here and I got curious, that's all. I wanted to see what it did, that's all."

"Sure. I know you ain't stupid, Poley. You don't just play around with things unless you know what they are. And even I know what the hell that thing is. You were trying to flood out the whole fuckin' barraque."

"No! I just wanted to check it out. You really think I'd be crazy enough to do something like that? I live here too, you know. I was just checking things out, that's all. Never know when I might find some kind of use for it."

"Okay. Flyte?"

"Well, I was down here . . . "

"What the fuck were you doing down here?"

"I, uh, I was just nosin' around, lookin' for some place to hide a few things, you know?"

"Yeah, and I know just what the hell you were tryin' to hide too. I thought you'd taken that thing apart."

"I did. But . . . I'd like to put it back together again some day, you know?"

"I'm not sure I trust you any more than I trust Poley. Okay, so what happened?"

"I heard someone coming down the stairs so I hid behind that old generator over there. It was Poley. He went right to that old lock."

"You knew what it was?"

"Sure. It's obvious. He didn't spend much time but immediately started to try to open it."

"That's not true!" Poley yelled.

"You heard it. He tried to open it. I couldn't let him do that so I attacked him but he knocked me over and was going to kill me when Casey and Pawn showed up."

"Yeah." Red turned toward Casey and Pawn. "What about you guys? What were you doing down here?" Casey George and Demon Pawn started to move forward. "Stay right where you are. You first." He pointed his knife at Pawn.

"You know, Red, Casey and I could rush you right now and you wouldn't stand a chance."

Red grinned back. "Sure. But don't forget—I got Kip and Flyte at my back. And if you rushed me, Poley'd get away and I got a sneaky feelin' you guys don't want that."

"What if you let me take on Poley, alone, just me and him?" Casey said.

"Maybe I will. But first you got to tell me what you guys are doin' down here."

Pawn was quiet a moment. "Sure. Why not? We were hiding out from Poley and Walston. When I saw him come down here, I followed him."

"I thought you said you were hiding from him."

"Casey and him got in a little argument last night and Poley got the worst of it and . . . "

"That's the first time I ever heard of Poley getting the worst of anything."

"He jumped me," Poley growled. "Hit me from behind. Let me and Casey go at it together. I'm willin' to do that, as long as he's stripped like me and without a knife."

Casey grinned and started taking off his shirt.

"Wait a minute! I ain't finished yet. There's some things about all this that just don't fit together." Red looked at Casey. "What the hell did you jump Poley for in the first place? I mean, I could beat the shit out of him in a fair fight any day of the week but I still wouldn't want to tangle with him any more than I got to."

"He was . . . " Casey George stopped suddenly.

Poley grinned. "What's the matter? Afraid of telling me something I already know?" He looked at Green. "You're getting deep into something you don't want to know about, kid. I'd get out of here if I was you."

"Red, maybe we oughta listen," Kip said.

"You gonna wind up in The Tower if you keep it up." Poley's grin seemed to get wider and Kip felt a chill go through him.

"Flyte?"

"I wanta hear it."

"Okay, kid. It's your funeral. There was a break-in at the starship lab topside a couple of nights ago."

"So?"

"Casey George and his friends engineered it."

"You can't prove that."

"I don't have to. That's Walston's job. He thought Marshall Polansky was involved and he wanted him taken topside for questioning and I was in the process of doing just that when Casey knocked me out. Then they went rabbit." He looked at

Pawn. "And now I find out you're in with them. It figures. I knew someone with brains had to have something to do with it."

Casey started toward him but stopped when Red waved his knife at him. "I'm gonna tear that son of a bitch apart," he said, "and you can't stop me with that little toy of yours."

"He still ain't told me what he was doing down here."

"I told you, Red. He was going to flood the barraque." Flyte said.

"But why?"

"To . . . he wanted to flush them out." Flyte indicated Casey George and Demon Pawn. Poley looked at him sharply but said nothing.

"Kinda late for that now, isn't it?"

"Yeah. We can settle this right now, if you'll let us." Poley looked eagerly in Casey George's direction.

"All right. I want to watch this." Red motioned toward Demon Pawn. "Stand back."

Casey George stripped down to his shorts and the two men faced each other, one still grinning, the other grim-faced, the others forming a half-circle around them, where Red had placed them, Demon Pawn between Red Green and Kip, with the girl next to Kip, and Flyte Error next to Red. It wasn't a very safe arrangement and it made Kip even more nervous.

Poley flicked a piece of debris with his foot. "Can Casey and I put our shoes on?"

Green looked doubtful.

"Look, I don't want to lose because I stepped on a little piece of cement in my bare feet."

"I don't trust you, Poley."

"He's right," Casey George said. "We can't go around wrestling here in our bare feet."

"Okay. But nothing else. Kip. Toss 'em their shoes."

No longer barefoot, they circled each other and feinted several times, Casey reaching out with his longer arms and barely slapping Poley. Finally Casey tried to punch Poley in the stomach but Poley grabbed his wrist and twisted. Casey went down and pulled Poley's feet from under him. The two men rolled on the floor, ignoring the grit that scraped their skin, punching and trying to grab each other. Casey was the stronger and bigger of the two but Poley was more agile and experienced. It was an even match. Casey George was on top now but only for a moment as Poley squirmed away.

Caught up by the fight, Kip was startled when Bluebird cried out sharply. He turned to see Nick Skarys, a bouncer who worked at any bar that would hire him, with his hand on Bluebird's shoulder.

When Bluebird cried out sharply, everyone, including Casey George, turned to look. Poley took that moment to pick up his clothes and his knife then slashed out at Casey George, knocked Flyte Error down, and was out the door.

"Is he all right?" Flyte Error was standing in shock, looking at Casey George.

The man who had put his hand on Bluebird's shoulder moved to where Casey lay. "Give me some light!" he ordered and they brought their lamps over.

"Keep your dirty hands off me, Skarys," Casey said tightly.

"You're in no condition to be choosey."

Casey winced as the Skarys probed the wound.

"Tear me off a piece of his shirt, will you?"

When the men stood around dumbly, Bluebird went over to the pile of clothes and obeyed Skarys.

"You're lucky," Skarys said. Poley was in too much of a hurry to do you any real damage."

"Well, I guess he and I are even now."

"I'd get something for that, if I were you, before it gets infected, but this ought to keep you from bleeding to death until then." Skarys wrapped the strips around Casey's waist. "You won't be doing any heavy lifting for a while."

As Skarys stood back, Casey glared at the face of Marshall Polansky in the glow of the lamps. "What the hell are you doing up here?"

"I heard the noise and I got scared. What's going on?"

"Nothin'. Don't worry about it."

"If I were you," Skarys said, "I'd get as far away from here as I could. Whatever you think of me, I don't do nothing for them topside unless they ask me and sometimes not even then. You're in some kind of big trouble and Poley's gonna be back looking for you."

"Not if Pawn catches him."

"If Pawn catches him, Pawn's the one who's gonna be in trouble." Skarys turned to Bluebird. "Come on. The Lady sent me to get you."

Bluebird tried to break loose from him. "I'm not going anywhere with you. Who are you?"

"She's with me. I'll take care of her." Kip tried to pull her away from Skarys but he was floored with a powerful left-handed backhand slap from the big man.

Skarys reached into his pocket and slapped something to the back of her neck, flung the girl over his massive shoulders, and exited up the other stairway as Red knelt by Kip and sat him up.

Red watched as Skarys left, carrying the girl like a sack of rations. The girl wasn't blood; she could only come between Kip and him and Flyte. He'd seen it happen with others. Besides, he'd had a few run-ins with Skarys when the older man had been fronting the door at some club Red was trying to enter and Red had always come out second best. He wasn't ready yet to face him in a real drag-outer.

He knelt down by the stunned autar player and sat him up. "Why didn't you stop him?" Kip asked.

"Why don't you ask me something easy?" Red growled. "Like, why don't I stop a mountain?"

"But he's going to . . . Lord knows what he's going to do to her." Kip got to his feet. "We've got to stop him, Red."

"Don't worry about Skarys. He's straight," Casey said from the doorway.

"Where are you going?" Red asked.

"After Poley." Casey disappeared into the darkness and Polansky stumbled after him. Kip started toward the doorway that Skarys had taken but Red easily stopped him.

"He said something about The Lady," Red said. "Has she got something to do with all this?"

"Maybe. I don't know. Come on." Kip finally broke free and ran out of the room and up the stairs without checking to see if his friends were following him.

Flyte Error looked at Red as Kip went out the doorway and up the stairs. "What'll we do?"

Red spread his hands in a gesture of futility. "What can we do? He's blood, ain't he? Let's go." Red started after Kip.

"Wait a minute. I . . . I'll stay here."

Red put a hand heavily on Flyte's shoulder. "He's your blood too. Come on." This time Flyte followed.

Pawn reached the top of the first flight of stairs but Poley was gone. Light filtered down the stairwell from the ground floor above. There was no sound. Poley didn't have that much of a head start—if he'd continued up the stairway, Pawn should still be able to hear him.

Pawn crouched down, making himself still closer to the ground as he moved into the first room off the stairwell. Poley's foot caught him in the shoulder but he was ready and rolled with it, coming up in a crouch as Poley, already dressed again, came at him. Pawn was able to dodge Poley's knife and sent him against a wall with his shoulder, where Poley's blade snapped.

Nursing the knuckles he had bruised against the wall, Poley waited as Pawn stalked him. "Come on. I know things you never dreamed of in the streets of the barraque."

Poley's grin angered Pawn and he thrust at him with his own knife. Poley grabbed his wrist and twisted but Pawn held desperately to the blade.

"Tough little bastard, aren't you?"

Pain erupted through Pawn's groin as Poley's knee caught him squarely between the legs, and Pawn dropped to his knees, one hand clutching his lower stomach while he somehow managed to hang on to the knife and keep it pointing in Poley's direction.

Poley shoved Pawn to the ground with a foot to the shoulder, making the pain scream even louder. Poley grinned. "I like your style, kid, but I don't have time to teach you any more. But don't worry. I'll be back. I ain't finished with you guys yet."

As Poley raced up the stairway, Pawn got to his feet and staggered after him but he had to stop at the foot of the stairs, doubled over as he grasped the rusty railing. That was the way Casey George and Marshall Polansky found him when they finally came up the stairway.

So Skarys was coming back to the barraque with Bluebird. Lady Madonna felt some relief but she knew things weren't over yet. The girl would wake up before Skarys got here and then he would have a hellion on his hands. And there were still the unanswered questions. What was Bluebird doing down there in the first place? Well, that was obvious—but how had she met Kip Marten? She hadn't found him when she had gone to the Oyster. What was going on down there? Why had the computer shown her that unexpected view? Something important was happening and she had no idea what it could be. All right then. It was time to put a worm into files she had sworn she would never touch.

"We've got to get upstairs," Pawn gasped.

"You're in no condition to tangle with Poley," Casey said. "Come on. You know these tunnels. Get us somewhere else."

"I can't." Pawn straightened up. "Stay here. You got a knife?"

"Yeah. But it's too dangerous here. Where you going? I'm coming with you."

"I've got to meet someone. He won't like it if I'm not alone." Pawn started up the stairway and Casey followed him.

"What about me?" Marshall whined.

"Everything's falling apart," Pawn muttered. "Everything's falling apart."

Kip was almost to the switch in the fence when Red caught up to him. He tried to shrug off Red's hand but the heavier man hung on. "Quit acting stupid, Kip."

"I've got to get her. You don't understand, Red."

"I understand you're acting like an asshole over a woman."

"She's not just a woman."

"Okay, okay." Red sighed and followed Kip under the fence. Flyte Error came last. "You ever wonder how that sonofabitch got in and out of here?"

"Which sonofabitch?"

"All of them. It doesn't matter which one."

"How the hell should I know? I don't care."

"Yeah, we had a real convention in there, didn't we? What about you, Flyte? How do you think they got in?"

"They all got connections one way or another. Poley works for Walston and Skarys works for Poley. We're barely worth stepping on to them."

They reached the main street and could see Skarys

hotfooting it ahead of them. He looked to Kip as if he was more than half a klick away.

"What're you gonna do when you catch up with him, Kip?"

"I don't know. I'll worry about it then. You got any ideas?"

"Yeah. He figures he can handle all three of us and he might be right. But he can't do it while he's got his arms around her. And she's going to be waking up pretty soon."

"So?"

"So, me and Flyte will keep him busy while you pick up the tuft and split."

"That the best you can do?" Kip asked.

"You got anything better?"

"No," Kip admitted glumly.

"It might work, " Flyte said. "It just might work."

"You really think so?" Kip asked.

Red snorted. "Don't listen to him. You know he's light in the head."

Kip thought about the device that he and Flyte had used. He didn't agree with Red at all but there was no use saying anything. Flyte was quiet except for his usual smile when Red said things about him.

Poley slowed down as soon as he was outside the fence. Whatever else happened, he wasn't going to be followed by Casey George. Not for very long, anyway. He wasn't worried about the kids—Skarys had effectively taken up their interest, as if he and Skarys had planned it between them. He had no idea what the bouncer had been doing there but that wasn't important—he'd find out from Skarys later, after everything had settled down.

That left only Demon Pawn and Poley didn't think he would abandon Casey George. So once he was out of the immediate area, he would be free and clear.

Before he had crossed the cleared area and could hide himself in one of the nearby buildings, he saw Skarys leave the warehouse with the girl limp on his shoulder. He stopped at the gate, fumbled with something a moment, then passed through without ever setting the girl down.

Poley smiled. Trust Skarys to have his own disrupter. Skarys would not care to have it known that he had one, so that gave Poley a little more edge over the bouncer. It was useful knowledge and it would be more useful if Poley could find out where he had gotten it.

Poley entered the closest building and quickly climbed to the second floor, past rusting girders and bricked-up windows. Skarys was nearly across the cleared area by the time Poley had gotten to his post. He was moving fast. Let him go. Poley had more important things to worry about.

He turned his attention back to the Ultimate Warehouse. Neither Casey George nor Demon Pawn appeared. Instead, the three young musicians came from around one side of the warehouse and started after Skarys, still arguing among themselves. Let them go too. Skarys could handle all three of them and maybe several more just like them and, if he couldn't, that was his problem, not Poley's.

From his perch, Poley could see the entire front of the warehouse and most of two sides. No one could escape from the building without his eventually seeing them . . . unless they went back down. Either that or the river.

Poley checked himself. He had left his flash back in the warehouse as well as one of his knives but he still had two knives and a couple of trank patches. It wasn't much but it really was all he needed.

Unwillingly, he started back to the warehouse. If they had gone back down to the tunnels, he wasn't going to follow them. But he still had the option of opening the floodgate.

Pawn managed to talk Casey and Marshall into waiting

for him on the second floor of the warehouse, overlooking the streets of Westmeat. The climb up two flights of stairs with a stiffening wound had helped convince Casey to let Pawn meet the messenger alone.

It was hard to believe that less than an hour had passed since Pawn had been signaled from across the river. So much had happened in such a brief time. Everything had changed.

He reached the smaller warehouse and looked around, seeing no one. He hoped it wasn't already too late. By his reckoning, he still had two or three minutes to go but he didn't really trust his timer. It would be just like them for the messenger to show up at one hour exactly and wait only a few seconds.

He walked around the corner of the building, out of sight of anyone in the Ultimate Warehouse. Surely someone should be here by now. But where exactly? The message, by its very simplicity, had not been that explicit.

A door behind him opened. "In here," a voice whispered as Pawn turned.

Pawn took out his knife and pushed the door open a little wider, moving in slowly and pressing his back against the wall to one side of the door. It closed behind him and he was in darkness.

"Can we have some light?" he asked.

"No." Pawn felt the pit of his stomach become hard, as if a cancer were growing inside. The voice, though disguised, was unmistakably feminine. "Listen carefully. You will have to remember all this."

"Things have changed."

There was a long moment while the messenger digested this. It was just like them, Pawn thought, not to realize that everything could go haywire in a moment.

"How have things changed?"

Pawn described what had happened in the Ultimate subbasement and how Casey was wounded and might not be able to move swiftly or for very long. "His wounds are growing stiff now. He's going to be hurting bad."

"That is the least of our problems," the voice said. "You said that Poley was trying to flood the barraque?"

"It sure looked that way to me. He was probably trying to flood us out so he could have his crack at Casey. But now that score's been evened."

"And this young man . . . this Flyte Error? . . . knew about it as well. That's odd."

"Flyte's odd. They all are."

"Wait a minute."

"Look, let's get this over with." There was no answer. "Hey, are you there?" Pawn reached into his pocket for his flash but it was on the floor of the Ultimate Warehouse. He felt around the wall, past the door, until he came to another corner. Then another corner, another corner, and soon he was back at the door. He was in a small anteroom, so small two people could hardly be in it without touching each other. He took a step forward in the dark, holding his hand out in front of him. Four steps and he could touch the opposite wall.

"When you leave, pick up the medication that will be on the floor. This should help Casey ignore his pain unless he is in far worse shape than you describe."

"What medication?"

"Come back to this building and wait on the top floor. You will be able to see svana as it forms outside the fence."

"Svana? Here?"

"Tonight. We have moved up the date. You will find costumes on the top floor. Put them on and join the svana immediately. Someone will be waiting for you at the gate. He will give you further instructions."

"That's all? For Lord's sake . . . " The door swung open and the afternoon light stabbed into Pawn's dark-accustomed eyes. There was no one in the tiny anteroom that was just as small as Pawn had determined. There seemed to be no other door to the room. On the floor at his feet were two packages.

She was being rocked like a little child, still dozing away in her bed, before her mother had died. But the movement was jolting and vaguely uncomfortable and people were shouting and yelling around her. Then the rocking stopped and she was jolted roughly and unceremoniously dropped to the ground. "Hey!" she shouted.

"Shhh!" someone said and grabbed her by the arm and pulled her to her feet. "Come on," he whispered, "we've got to get out of here."

She tried to wipe the cobwebs out of her mind. She knew this young man but ... "Kip!" she said suddenly as things began to click into place. "What's happening? What's going on?"

"Come on!" He yanked her arm and started running. "We got no time for explanations."

She followed him, trusting him because she had no choice and because she wanted to trust him anyway, wanted to believe in him. Behind them there were angry shouts and grunts. She recognized Red Green's voice. It seemed high and excited and happy.

"This way."

She followed Kip over a mound of powdered concrete with pieces of brick and board sticking out, then down the other side, past piles of fire-blackened wood, tires, ashes, twisted rusting pipes and jagged strips of metal, past decaying mattresses and animals, into a gaping doorway and down a flight of stairs, past startled old men and women, then down a dark and slimy corridor lit only by Kip's flash, with unknown horrors lurking in the dark unlit shadows.

They finally reached the basement of another building and stopped at the bottom of a stairwell, gasping and trying to regain their breaths. Light streamed down from above.

"Kip ... Kip ... " She stopped, trying to get enough breath to finish her sentence. "What's happening?"

"I don't ... really know. ... All that stuff in the warehouse?

. . . I don't know . . . what it was about."

"I've got to get home. The Lady . . . "

"I'll take you."

"No!" She gripped his arm. "If The Lady saw you and me together . . . "

"I'll take you, " Kip said firmly. "You're my woman now," he sang but she didn't recognize the song.

"I'm not your woman," she said strongly. "I'm not anybody's woman but my own."

Kip grinned. "Okay, okay. You ready? Let's go." He started back up the stairway.

Polansky returned from his watch on the other side of the building at the same time that Casey saw Pawn coming back from the small riverside warehouse. "Poley's coming back," Polansky said.

That was information Casey could do without. He got up and almost doubled over from the pain in his side. "Come on. Let's go," he said through clenched teeth. He wasn't going to let the pain get the best of him and he certainly wasn't going to show Marshall Polansky how much pain he was in.

Yet he had to stop several times when they started down the stairway, feeling as if he was going to pass out. Pawn met them before they got to the ground floor. He took one look at Casey and told him to wait. Gratefully Casey stopped and waited as Pawn came up to him and slapped a patch on the back of his neck.

"What the hell'd you do?" Casey growled.

"Painkiller."

"Where'd you get it?"

"My contact give it to me. Let's move."

"You trust him?"

"We have to."

Even now, Casey could feel the warmth spreading through

his body as the chemical coursed through his arteries and veins. The pain in his side became a distant thing, never quite gone, always there to warn him if he went too far, but able to be ignored for the time being. He was getting light-headed and messages from all his senses seemed to come from a distance. He didn't like that but that was the price he had to pay for freedom from his pain and the mobility that otherwise would be lost.

"Where we goin'?" he asked.

"Not far."

"Poley's returning. Marshall told me."

"Let's move it then."

They raced across the broken field of rubble that separated the warehouse from the smaller building. Casey felt like he was floating, despite the occasional twinges of pain that managed to get through the drug's effects.

When they got to the building, Pawn swore.

"What's the matter?" Casey asked.

"This door. It's where I talked to the messenger. It's locked."

"What about this one?" Polansky pointed to another door further down the wall.

That door opened readily and they found themselves in a well-lit medium-sized room, although there were no windows and no immediate obvious source for the light. Pawn headed for the stairway going up one wall.

"Where you going?"

"To the top floor. That's where my contact told us to go."

"You really trust him, don't you?"

"It wasn't a him. It was a her."

"What'd she look like?"

"I don't know. I never saw her."

"You never saw her?" Casey's voice was practically a shout. "What were these, messages from heaven?"

Pawn patiently told him what had happened as they climbed the stairway to the third and final floor. There was no entrance to the second floor.

"I don't like it," Casey said. "I don't like it at all."

"We don't have a hell of a lot of choice," Pawn said wearily.

"I wish you'd quit saying that."

The third floor was stacked with boxes, all in neat rows and piles. Over one box were the costumes that the voice had told Pawn about. Casey sat down on one of the boxes, feeling as if he would break in two at any minute. Despite the painkiller, he was exhausted and hurting. "This must have been where she was," he said. "She probably got out as soon as you left. You should've stuck around a while longer and nabbed her."

"And left you to deal with Poley?"

"I can handle him."

"Yeah, I've noticed. As long as he's got his back to you."

"Listen, you little . . . " Casey grabbed Pawn by the back of his shirt then dropped him. "I'm sorry. I'm on edge."

"We're all on edge," Pawn said, apparently unperturbed. "Marsh. Keep an eye out those windows for Poley."

"Right."

"You closed the door downstairs, didn't you?"

"I think so," Casey said.

"Better go down and check."

"Look, Pawn, I'm not your goddamned errand boy!"

"All right, all right! I'll do it." For the first time, a note of irritation entered Pawn's voice.

"Forget it, forget it. I'm sorry. Okay?" Casey started down the stairway. He could feel the muscles around his wound screaming at him distantly and he knew he was going to feel pretty bad when the 'killer wore off but he'd deal with that when the time came.

The door was closed. "Fuckin' Pawn," he muttered under his breath as he checked it. The door would not open. There was no knob or lock, just a simple fixed handle. "Shit!" After several more attempts to open it, Casey gave up and looked around the room. To his right would be the room that Pawn had first entered. There was just a wall there, no two-way mirror or anything else: just a blank, unadorned wall. The doorway at the back of the room led to a narrow, dark, musty hall. Casey took out his flash. There was no indication that anyone had been there in quite a while. At the end of the corridor was a plain door with no handle or sign of a lock. It wouldn't push open.

This was it, of course. This was the room from which the woman had observed Pawn and talked to him. Maybe she was in there right now.

He braced himself against the opposite wall and kicked out at the door. His wound screamed but Casey was sure he had felt the door give a little. He closed his eyes and waited for the pain to die down. His exertions had taken more out of him than he had expected. He realized that he had very little left in reserve, but he had enough for at least one more kick and that was all he needed. The door swung open violently and smashed against something. The room inside was dark. Casey leaned over to pick up his flash and the pain struck. Muscles that had been cut and abused could take no more, painkiller or no painkiller, and Casey went to his knees, waiting for the waves of pain to end.

When they were finally bearable after an eternity that was probably less than thirty seconds, Casey, still on his knees, pointed his flash into the room. There were wires and conduits neatly strung up and down its walls; something that looked like a pneumatic tube from one of the factories crossed at slightly over head height and disappeared in the far wall. It was small, even smaller than the room that Pawn had described, two steps from doorway to opposite wall, four at most in width. It was nothing more than an electronics closet. Someone could hide in here, yes, as Pawn himself had done during their raid, but it would be cramped and uncomfortable quarters.

"What the hell's going on down here?" Pawn's voice cut through his thoughts. "What was all that noise?"

"Look at this, Pawn." Casey gestured toward the closet. "Here's where your contact must have been."

Pawn laughed. "Lord, Casey, is that what you've been doing down here? I hope no one could hear you outside. Come on." Pawn helped Casey to his feet and moved slowly down the hallway, Casey leaning on Pawn, pain stabbing at him with every step. "Look at you. You're bleeding again." Dumbly Casey looked at the bright red stain spreading on his shirt. "Think you can make it upstairs?"

"Yeah." Casey wasn't as sure as he tried to make it sound, however.

"There was no one in the closet, Case." Casey said nothing. "There was no one else in the whole building but me. It was all transmitted here from over the river."

"What about the 'killers?"

"They probably stocked this place months ago. The dispenser's upstairs. Anything we want or need, Casey."

"If they know so fuckin' much, man, why the hell didn't they stop Poley?"

Flyte wasn't happy about it. He wasn't a fighter, not like Red. He relied on his brains and knowledge. Even Kip was better with his fists and a knife than Flyte was. But he waded in nonetheless, striking against Skarys's waist and legs like a terrier nipping at its quarry's heels and Red pummeled him one on one while Kip dragged the girl away. Skarys knew what they were up to immediately but it took him the better part of a minute to swat Green off his feet and considerably less to take care of Flyte. By that time Kip and the girl were gone. Skarys took one step, looked around, then picked up Green by the front of his shirt and snarled, "Where are they going?"

Red laughed. "I have no idea. We hadn't thought that far ahead."

Skarys looked at him for a long hard moment then threw him back to the ground. He leaned over to pick up Flyte, who tried to scramble away. "It's true, it's true. We just wanted to get her away from you."

To Flyte's surprise, Skarys stopped and grinned. "Well,

what the hell. I've done everything The Lady asked me to."
He helped Flyte to his feet then shoved him up against a wall.
"Now get the hell out of here before I lose my temper."

Flyte looked at Red, who nodded. Flyte started to run but
Red grabbed him as roughly as Skarys had and slowed him down
to a walk. "Don't give the bastard the satisfaction," he said in a
low voice.

Flyte looked back. Skarys was still standing there, glaring
at them.

"What're we gonna do?"

They turned a corner and Red raced over to an abandoned
building. "Come on. Don't stand there like a dummy."

Flyte followed him to the next floor. "What're you
doing?"

"Don't tell me you trust that bastard. You think he's going
to give up that easy?"

"But what can he do? Kip's gone. Do you have any idea
where he went?"

"No. That's why Skarys let us go. He realized we weren't
going to be any help."

"But he said . . . "

"I know what he said! He was just trying to get rid of us so
he could go after Kip."

"I don't understand."

"You don't understand nothing, pussy. Look."

Skarys appeared in the street below them, walking slowly,
looking. He passed underneath them so slowly that Flyte was
afraid he would see them above him or even hear their breathing.
Halfway down the block, he stopped and walked back. Red
pulled Flyte away from the open window and they moved toward
the other side of the building, Red keeping them back just far
enough that they could see the top of Skarys's head as he turned
the corner and walked slowly down the side street.

They inched forward, keeping him in sight until he stopped
at the alley alongside the building, stood a moment before
walking over to the pile of rubble to examine it closely then

smiled to himself and climbed quickly over it. They jerked back as he looked up at the building on the other side of the alley then watched him enter.

"Shit," Red said softly.

"What'll we do now?" Flyte asked.

"I don't know. I just don't know."

Pawn looked at Casey George sleeping the sleep of the exhausted in one corner of the top floor of the small building. He had barely been able to make it up the stairs and had passed out while Pawn was cleaning his wound again, cauterizing and sealing it with the supplies in the top floor's dispenser. It was as if the upper echelons of the movement had known exactly what they would need and when. But the dispenser had probably been here for months and undoubtedly there were others scattered through the barraque that would never get used at all.

"Is he going to be all right?" Marshall asked.

"He'll survive if we do."

"What do you mean?"

"Marsh, it'll be dark in a couple of hours. Tonight is the night of svana and the parade . . . "

"How do you know?"

"For Lord's sake, Marsh, weren't you listening? My contact told me. I told you that."

"But how did she know?"

"How would I know? Probably a couple of people in the upper circle of the movement are also in the upper svana circles."

"But a woman?"

"Lord, Marsh, this isn't one of your damned religious deals. We're working on a revolution and your sacred rituals are just going to have to be violated a little bit."

"I don't like it."

"Tough. It's too late."

Pawn turned away from the argument to look out of one of the narrow windows toward the Ultimate Warehouse. Poley was in there now, looking for them. When would he think of coming over here to check out this building? Would he be able to break into it somehow? Did they have enough time? Exactly where would svana begin? His contact had said it would be outside this building but suppose it was outside the fence. How could they get through it to join svana? They didn't have Poley's resources. Perhaps there was a key up here. But wouldn't his contact have said something about that? Was this some kind of a test for them, for him? There were too damn many questions and too few answers.

Somewhere the upper circles of the movement intersected the upper circles of svana. The original message had said that svana would be tomorrow night but when they had learned of Casey's wound and the problems inside the old Ultimate Warehouse, suddenly svana was to be tonight. Pawn was certain he had gotten the first message correct. The wheels were turning and tomorrow he, Marsh, and Casey would be on their way to a new life. Either that or they would be dead or in The Tower. He didn't really look forward to any of the choices; starting a new life somewhere else among strangers, without all the friends he had accumulated in a lifetime in the barraque, so much of his knowledge useless, was not a prospect to be relished much more than the alternatives. It probably would kill Marsh but Pawn had no idea how it would affect Casey. He wondered if it all was really worth it.

Meanwhile there was nothing to do but wait and think. Somewhere near him, preparations for svana were going full blast but Pawn could see no sign of the activity. The old Ultimate Warehouse would have been a perfect place for such preparations but it had been left alone, perhaps because Kip Marley and his friends were using it.

And what about the building they were in right now? The only signs of svana were the costumes they were to wear. There had been no entry to the second floor, other than a brief corridor from one stairway to the next. Maybe there was a trap door under these heavy boxes. Pawn thought of moving things around to try to find out but he didn't have the energy. Perhaps he should ask Marshall to try—it would keep him busy but he probably didn't have much strength left either and Pawn didn't relish the thought of Polansky collapsing from exertion.

"Pawn? Are we really going to leave the barraque?"

"I don't know, Marsh. We don't have time to worry about such things now. Let's take an inventory of this place, see if we can find any weapons or something we can use as a weapon. We have no idea what's going to go down tonight and we still have Poley to worry about."

One thing they wouldn't have to worry about was medication and drugs. There were enough stimulants in the dispenser to keep them awake for a year.

It had not been easy. She had had to move from one file to another, break its lock, find another and then another until suddenly, in a burst of associations, it had all become clear. Thread after thread had been added in an apparently meaningless jumble until suddenly and unexpectedly there was a beautiful pattern visible in the tapestry of data. Yet all one had to do was pull one thread and it would all unravel. And now Bluebird had inadvertently put herself into the pattern.

The key to everything was the break-in at the starship lab: that had been hidden from her before, something she had never suspected. Then the discovery of Marshall Polansky's DNA, which led to Casey George, and finally Poley was on his way to the Ultimate Warehouse in an attempt to drown Casey George and Polansky, which, as a side effect, would also probably destroy a large section of Westmeat. That Kip Marten and his friends were using the Warehouse and so would also probably be caught by the destruction was just another side effect, into which Bluebird had tumbled.

But now she was safely in Skarys's hands and out of danger. The next question was what Poley was doing in the Warehouse, since he apparently had decided not to drown Westmeat, at least not just yet. She had to protect her people there; she was spending too much time worrying about Bluebird and letting her duties to the barraque slip. She tried to contact people but most of the men to whom she wanted to talk were unavailable, which was very strange indeed.

She finally talked to the tender at the Oyster. "Yeah, a bunch of them were here," she said, "but then one of the factory workers came in about an hour or so ago and talked to them. I don't know what he said but they finished their drinks in a hurry and left."

The story was the same at nearly every bar she contacted, with men leaving in a hurry when someone came in with a message. It could mean only one thing but that was unheard of—svana was being moved up. That had never happened before.

She called Gloria's home. "Yes, my lady?"

"Please send someone to tell your grandmother that there is danger in Westmeat tonight."

"There is no danger, my lady."

"Tell her there is. Tell her that Poley is inside the Ultimate Warehouse."

"Yes, my lady. But there is no danger."

If only she could rush down there herself, make them all see it. But she could not. It would be wrong. No woman, not even Lady Madonna, could interfere with svana.

Skarys was on Kip's trail. He wouldn't be hampered or slowed down by the girl anymore so it wouldn't take him long to catch up with them. There was no time to waste. Red jumped out the window onto the back of the bouncer. The jolt knocked Skarys to the ground but Red thought he felt something break, a rib probably, and he had the wind knocked out of him. But he had no time to worry about that: Skarys was getting up again. Red grabbed a piece of brick and smashed it against the back of the bouncer's head. Skarys pitched forward on his face and lay still, a trickle of bright red blood coming from where Red had hit him.

Now Red had time to get his breath but the pain in his chest made it difficult each time he tried to inhale. By the time he was finally able to get his breath without too much pain, Flyte had climbed down from the second floor.

"You didn't kill him, did you, Red?"

"Nah. I doubt it. He's got a hard head. He'll be okay when he comes around but he's gonna be hurting. And he's really gonna have a grudge against us now. Check him out."

Gingerly, Flyte examined the bouncer. "I guess he's okay. He's breathing and his heart's beating okay."

Doily poked his head up over a pile of debris. "I thought I saw you kids. What you up to, Red?"

"Doily. Just the man I wanted to see."

"That sounds like bad news. See ya."

"Come here!"

Doily grinned and climbed over the pile. While not as burly as Skarys, he probably could have done better against him in a fight than Red, even allowing for the fact one of his arms had been amputated at the elbow.

"You got something for me, kid?"

"Yeah. I want you to watch him for me."

Doily looked down at Skarys's inert form. "Oh, Lord, you really got yourself into trouble this time, didn't you? You're really in trouble now and there ain't no way I can help you."

"All I want you to do is keep him from following Kip."

"Sure. Me and what army? You may not like livin' so much, kid, but I still do. Count me out."

"Hey, look, I'll owe you big. I promise."

"Sure. We both gonna have a price on us. How the hell'm I gonna collect when I'm lying in a ditch somewheres with my skull split open?" Doily looked down at Skarys again. "Boy, how'd you do that to him, kid? You know somethin' I don't know?" Red lifted the piece of brick. "Oh, shit, man, you cheated. That's no fair."

"It's what you taught me, Doily."

"Sure, but . . . you don't do shit like that to guys like Sharys. He'll have your ass fried three ways from Sunday."

"Look, he's after Kip. Can't you help us?"

"What're you goin' to be doin' while I'm gettin' the shit beat out of me?"

"Catch up with Kip and protect him."

"What's he need protection for?"

"Skarys is after him."

"Why?"

"He's got a tuft with him."

"That don't compute, Red. Skarys don't get serious over no tuft."

"I think he was supposed to protect her or somethin'."

"Okay, okay. I'll stay here and talk with Mister Skarys. I'd rather tangle with him than someone or something he's supposed to be protectin' someone from." Doily looked down again at Skarys's still form. "I think. But I ain't gonna put my ass in a sling for you. I'll slow him down a little bit but that's all I promise."

"Great. Let's glide, Flyte."

The room was empty. This time Poley checked behind every piece of machinery. Something about this didn't ring right. Casey George had left blood stains at one spot on the floor of the room but none anywhere else. An autar lay on the floor. The room and the stairway leading up was a mess—the debris and the dust had been disturbed by too many people to try to make any sense out of it. But the dust on the stairway leading down from this subbasement was still undisturbed. Poley checked the other to find numerous footprints going in both directions—it was probably the route that Casey, Pawn, and Polansky had taken from the lowest subbasement while Nick Skarys had taken that staircase down.

They hadn't gone back down, that was clear, so there was no need any longer for Poley to open the flood gate. It was too late for that. But something inside him made him want to open the damn thing up and watch it destroy part of the barraque. He was filled with an anger that threatened to consume him—he was angry at Casey George; he was angry at Benj Walston; he was angry at Lady Madonna; and he was angry at every living soul in the barraque, at the world itself. He was almost out of control and perhaps the only thing that kept him from opening the gate was the knowledge that he would probably be his own first victim.

So if they hadn't gone down and burrowed under the barraque again to rise up in some other abandoned building somewhere, where could they have gone? He couldn't search every single floor of the whole building. It would be too easy for them to avoid him and then leave when he had reached the top of the building, unable to do anything but stand up there and watch them get away.

He looked at the control wheels. There had to be a way to open it without endangering himself. The designer certainly wouldn't have made the whole thing into a suicide trap. There had to be a sequence or perhaps a timer built in. Would it still be operable after all these years?

He was crazy to even be thinking about it. It wasn't as easy as he had thought it would be when he had been sitting in his room listening to the puter talk to him and Benj Walston.

He climbed slowly back to the ground floor, stopping frequently to listen, hearing nothing but the peeping of sparrows, the cooing of pigeons, and the faint sounds of the river and Westmeat. As he neared the top he was able to distinguish a few distant voices but he recognized none of them.

He carefully examined each of the small rooms on the

ground floor until he finally stopped, mesmerized briefly by the view out the empty window frame. The river! Of course. He had been so blind. They could have taken a small boat and crossed to the other side or even gone up or down the river on this side. That, in fact, was more likely—they hadn't had enough time to cross the river and he could see nothing like a small boat in the river, although there were large chunks of debris that he had to watch closely before he realized they were moving with the current. Even as he watched, several of them were gobbled up by a rivercleaner, another reason for them to avoid trying to cross.

Then he noticed the smaller building between the warehouse and the river and the footsteps in the mud leading from the Ultimate Warehouse toward the smaller building. He crossed the space between the two buildings quickly and without incident, then stopped and pressed himself against the wall and waited. Nothing happened. The only sounds were those of the birds and the clatter of the rivercleaners, the distant shouts of ragpickers, and the splashing of waves against the breakwall.

One set of footprints in the mud led back to the Ultimate Warehouse but the rest went only in this one direction. The building was surrounded by a wide concrete lip; a few clumps of half-dried mud might be an indication of their presence but it was uncertain. A jumble of rock and brick and rusted machinery lay under the first floor, which was raised some distance off the ground. There were no footprints going toward the river.

The building was lined up so well with the warehouse that he could easily have seen anyone leave from either end. Something about this arrangement bothered Poley but he couldn't figure out just what it was. He would just have to let it keep nibbling at his subconscious until it identified itself.

He looked at the warehouse again: it was really remarkable how well they lined up—the center of the warehouse was in a line with the center of the smaller building. It probably only meant that they were built at the same time . . . and yet . . .

The door nearest him opened easily onto a stairway going

up to the second floor. Light filtering in from the windows above made it easy to see the clean-swept stairs that showed no footprints. The building had obviously been in use recently.

The door closed behind him and shut itself with a solid click. Poley tested it—it was locked. He had walked right into a trap. How could he have been so dumb?

They would be expecting him to come up the stairs slowly so he raced up them as lightly and quietly as he could . . . to discover an empty room, light flowing in through large windows on three sides. The fourth was walled off securely and all the windows were fully paned with glass that was reinforced with wire mesh.

He was trapped, taken completely out of action. Poley took out his heaviest knife and used the handle to smash a couple of windows. It took a while to pry out the tiny jagged pieces of glass but soon there was a flow of air in the room. At least they wouldn't be able to gas him.

He sat down with his back against the fourth wall. That was when he heard, faintly but clearly, the sound of footsteps going up a stairway that had to be behind him, and the voice of Demon Pawn cajoling. He could make out Casey's name several times. Then he heard them walking around above him, moving things. So near and yet so far. Had they heard him breaking the window? Apparently not. They seemed too relaxed for that.

Poley looked around his prison again. There had to be a way out of here but there wasn't a piece of furniture or a box in the room, nothing. He must have missed something—they couldn't have cleaned it out so completely. Except for that one wall, everything else had been stripped to the support beams, which stood out against the outer wall. There wasn't an electrical fixture or a wire; if there were any in the building, they had been routed behind the wall. It was as if they had been expecting him and knew that he would never be carrying a cell.

He walked over to the stairway. It was dark now, in shadow, with the door closed but, in the ceiling high above him, too far away to reach, he could see the lens of a minicam pointed in the direction of the doorway. How long would it be before Casey George was notified that he was imprisoned beneath him? He wished they knew right now. Casey George would try to find some way to reach him and then Poley could be free once again.

There was no way around it; there was only one thing he could think of to do. He went to one of the windows whose glass he had broken, took his knife out again, and hit the window over and over again until the glass was shattered all the way to the frame. Then he picked at it with his knife until he could get at the wire and starting sawing at it with his blade. It would take a lot of time and he would ruin a good knife but there was no sense in just waiting for something to happen.

"Where are we going?"

"I'm taking you home."

"Home?"

"To The Lady. That's where you belong, isn't it?"

"I don't belong to her. I never did. I only thought I did." She was quiet a moment then said so softly Kip could barely hear her, "If I belong with anyone, I belong with you, Kip."

Kip stopped for a moment and looked at her. She wanted to cry for the sadness in his eyes. "No. You can never belong to me. You could no longer belong to me than a 'quiste could belong to the starship."

"You could, Kip. You could."

"No. And I wouldn't want to." He took her by the wrist and pulled her painfully along.

"You're hurting me!"

"Well, come along then. Or would you rather wait for Skarys?"

"We're safe from him, aren't we?"

"We'll be safe from him when we get to The Lady's and not until then."

He slowed down at last, so she could keep up with him without being yanked along. Night was coming; the pigeons and sparrows had given the sky to nightbirds, strange ugly creatures that uttered faint squawks that were barely audible. They seemed so graceful up there in the darkened sky as they swooped after insects but she remembered one she had found dying on a rooftop, an ungainly creature that flopped around helplessly and hissed at her through a huge gaping mouth.

"Kip?"

"What?" He made no attempt to keep the irritation out of his voice.

"I left your autar back in that building. I'm sorry."

"That's all right."

"I really am sorry."

"Look, we've got more important things to worry about right now. Can't you hurry it up a little?"

"Can't you let me stop and catch my breath?"

"In a little while. We've got to put some distance between us and Skarys while we can."

"Release the Speyes."

"It is early yet, Mister Secretary. They aren't due to be released for another twenty-two minutes and thirty seconds."

"Release them now."

Casey floated up from a deep dreamless sleep, feeling something cold and damp against the side of his neck. He reached up and pulled away a patch and found himself looking into Demon Pawn's face.

"How you feelin'?"

He moved and felt a sharp twinge of pain in his side. The rest of his muscles didn't seem too happy either. "Are you going to give me another 'killer?'"

"I already did but not as strong as the last one. You need to have your wits about you."

Casey slowly got to his feet. He would be able to live with the pain. While he had slept, Pawn had obviously bound his wound again, this time with a bandage that contained some knit-inducer. But there hadn't been time for very much repair, even with the accelerator. Before the night was through, the wound would probably be open again. But the pain of that thought was lessened by the knowledge that soon they would be free. It would be worth it.

"Put on your costume. It's almost time."

Gray light filtered through the windows and the entire room was in shadow. Marshall Polansky was just a lumpy shape in the gloom.

Casey looked out the window as he put on the gawdy pants and shirt. He looked at the feathered hawk-mask; he rather liked it.

"Here. You better hang onto these in case you need them."

Casey took the patches and bandage packs from Pawn and stuffed them into his shirt. They made a bit of a bulge and he looked fatter than he actually was but that wouldn't fool the infrared of the flying spies.

"When do we leave?"

"As soon as we see some activity out there. It won't be long now."

Pawn had become some kind of animal, a weasel perhaps. Casey wouldn't know until he put on his mask. Marshall moved to look up at him and Casey found himself looking into the death's mask of a skull.

Kip kept looking behind them whenever he had the chance but he never saw anyone. That didn't mean much—Skarys could be circling around them and then they would meet him coming towards them. But Kip's pride wouldn't let the bouncer get his hands on Bluebird again, even if he was only going to deliver her to The Lady, just as Kip himself planned to do.

He didn't want to let go of Bluebird but there was no other choice, except to deal with Lady Madonna. He had managed to steer clear of anything that looked like law or power most of his life, if you ignored a couple of incidents with the squids that Red Green had initiated, and he had every intention of keeping it that way. He'd never heard of anyone who'd tangled with anyone in power who'd come out ahead.

But, damn it, he hated to let Bluebird go. She was . . . well, she really wasn't much to look at, kind of thin, kind of plain. But he remembered the way she had looked at him when she had handed him his autar after the drag-outer at the Money Marriage and well, hell, he guessed he was in love with her. No wonder Red was so upset. Well, one day he'd do the same, for all his talk of women being nothing but tufts whom he used for his own pleasure and then discarded. There'd been damn few of those anyway and the three of them all dreamed of the day when their band became so famous that they could pick and choose their women, toss them aside whenever they got tired of them, spiffies and 'quistes alike.

Well, it was all different now.

It was almost too dark to see anything. Where were they? When was this damned svana going to start?

"What are we waiting for?" Casey asked.

"Nothing. Let's go outside where we can see better." Pawn started for the stairway.

"What about Poley?"

"His eyes aren't any better than ours and we've all got knives."

"Wait a minute," Polansky said. "I saw something out

there."

Pawn rushed over to the window. "Where?"

"Over there." Polansky pointed toward the furthest part of Westmeat, where it came to an end against the stone wall and the river.

Were those shapes out there moving in the darkness or was it just imagination? It was probably just ragpickers. A light flared suddenly and briefly Pawn saw a group of men huddling over something that looked like a float of some kind. Or did he just want it to be one? It didn't matter. Marshall had seen it and he had seen it. It was all he needed to get them moving.

It took a while to get down the stairway in the dark, Casey moving much more slowly than Pawn would have wished. But eventually they got to the bottom and stood in the night air, the river pulsing against the bank only a few meters away, the building that had been their hideaway a dark bulk against the starless sky, illuminated dimly by the harsh red glare of the ceaseless fires across the river.

They turned toward the direction of the furthest reaches of the barraque when they heard Poley's voice calling Casey's name. Casey turned around, knife in hand. "Where are you?"

"Up here. On the second floor."

They looked up but could see nothing. Was this a trick?

"I'm trapped up here. I need your help to get out."

"Stay there," Casey said.

"What's the matter? Are you afraid of me?"

"I'm not afraid of you or anyone." Casey started to move back toward the building but Pawn stopped him.

"How do we know you're up there?" Pawn said. "We can't see a thing."

"Look in the center window." They saw a hand, dimly visible, reach out.

"So you're trapped. That's just tough, Poley. Someone'll get you out tomorrow, don't worry."

They walked toward the end of the barraque, leaving Poley cursing behind them.

"I'd like to nail that son of a bitch," Casey muttered.

"You're in no shape to nail anyone." Pawn felt nervous about Poley. He wasn't likely to stay put all night.

They reached the fence, sizzling softly in the night, at the edge of the warehouse grounds. "What do we do now?" Casey asked.

"Find a gate."

They started walking away from the river. A voice in the darkness said, "Stop." A flash shone briefly in their faces then gestured toward an open gate.

"How much time have we got?" Pawn asked.

"About five minutes."

"Wait for me. If I'm not back, go ahead without me."

"Pawn . . . " Casey was talking to empty air.

Pawn was already racing for the dark bulk of the Ultimate Warehouse. The knowledge that Poley was trapped in the other building had given Pawn an idea: he was going to make the agent pay for causing them so much trouble. He hoped that the kids weren't in the warehouse any longer but it really didn't matter to him whether or not they were. He tried to remember the sequence of instructions he had memorized so long ago when he had set down the map that was to have led others underground to the Ultimate Warehouse.

As soon as he was inside, he took out his flash and raced headlong down the stairs to the room where the floodgate was located. There was no time for finesse, no time for secrecy. If only he could remember the sequences accurately and if only everything still worked the way it was supposed to . . . that was a lot of ifs.

There were actually three locks in the system: one at the river bank, one inside the Ultimate Warehouse, and one between them, that was almost underneath the small building where Poley was trapped. All of them could be controlled from the room inside the Ultimate Warehouse.

Each system also had a built-in timer, which was controlled by one of the valves. All the way counterclockwise and it would be half an hour before the riverside lock would be activated. Two more valves counterclockwise told the timing system to open them. Then he set the valves for the middle lock. All of them were rusted and fought him as strongly as they had fought Poley but Pawn managed to turn them all the way and raced back out of the building. His palms felt like raw pieces of meat.

The light flashed in his face again and he ran through the gate.

"You didn't leave yourself much time," the voice said. "Come on."

The contact was covered with a black cloak but Pawn couldn't have made out his face in the darkness anyway. In a few moments, he joined Casey and Marshall.

"Over here. You." Their contact pointed to Marshall. "You're in the middle. The other two of you on either side of him. Follow this float." The contact jumped up on the platform in front of them. "I'll tell you what to do when the time comes."

"Casey," Pawn said. "Give me a couple of your bandages."

He wrapped his hands in them, waiting for the anaesthetic and the bactericide in them to take effect.

Poley had been certain that Casey George would have wanted to come up to the second floor and tear him apart. Then he would have been free.

He raced down the stairs and slammed his shoulder into the door. It was solid and wouldn't budge. He would fracture his shoulder before he'd break down that door. One of those beams might do the job but not his body.

He went back upstairs and went around the room testing all the supports to see if he could find one that was loose. He had no luck. He had expected none.

He stopped and looked out the shattered window toward the old warehouse. How many ways were there out of here?

There was the door and there were the windows. His hands were sore from the work he'd already done and his knife was ruined but it was still the most likely way that he could think of. He tore another strip from his shirt and wrapped it around his hand and began attacking the wire again. The knife no longer cut through it as easily as before but he figured he should be able to peel away a piece of the mesh large enough to get through in less than an hour.

They split up, Flyte following one route, Red another. Flyte thought it was hopeless but Red acted as if he knew what he was doing. How could they possibly find Kip; how could they know where he was going? He was obviously heading back to The Point but beyond that . . . who know? Maybe they would find him at The Oyster with Brookie and Libido, laughing at them, but Flyte seriously doubted that. Kip was frightened and he would have to go underground. But where? The warehouse was behind them and Flyte had a feeling they would never go back.

Well, whatever Red and Kip wanted to do, he would go back. That device, whatever it was, was still there in that big old vault and it was calling him back. He had told Red that he could put it back together and that was probably true—he had examined it carefully and he was confident he could have taken it apart and put it back together so it would work.

But he could never have built another one. There were too many parts that were obviously hand-made, one of a kind, priceless, and he had no idea how to make them.

Then he saw Red beckoning to him from a building across the street and he joined him.

"Look. I told ya, didn't I?"

In the street only a block and a half away, Flyte could see Kip and the girl moving quickly. But she was slowing Kip down. It wouldn't take long for Red and Flyte to catch up with them.

"Let's go," Flyte said eagerly.

"Slow down, Flyte, they don't know we're here and they don't need to know we're here."

"What're you talking about?"

"We'll just give 'em a little rear guard action, okay? Doily ain't gonna hold Skarys up very long and, if I can find 'em, then it oughta be a piece of concrete for Skarys, right?"

Flyte agreed. What he didn't say was that he saw no reason for both of them to be there. Red was worth two of Flyte in an action like this and Flyte wanted to be back in the vault. But there was no way he could say that to Red.

The night was split by light, the actinic lights of hundreds of high-powered lights held aloft on heavy poles carried by masked dockworkers, most of them stripped to the waist. Others walked beside them, ready to take over whenever a polebearer faltered.

For all the times that Casey had witnessed svana, for all the emotions it had evoked in his childhood, teen-aged, and adult breast, they were nothing compared to the electric thrill that shocked through him now, having found himself in the middle of the celebration, taking him completely by surprise.

Casey was not a particularly religious person, although he usually kept his scoffing to himself. Strong as he was, he would be no match for any of the lifelong barraquiste laborers, even those who were in their fifties. One didn't mock the beliefs of someone so much stronger than you, not if you wanted to keep your bones unbroken.

But standing here in that sudden light as the float ahead of them began to move forward, Casey felt an electric thrill of emotion that brought tears to his eyes.

"Start moving, you three," the voice of their contact said. "And make it look good. Make it look like you know what you're doing."

They began moving silently through Westmeat. Casey

could not see up to the bed of the float, where one of the chosen sat immovable in a pose as the Lord, perhaps in padmasana, perhaps standing with his arms outstretched in blessing, perhaps holding the thunderbolt of revenge that the barraquistes dreamt of, that would bring them to their rightful place in life and not merely the promised nirvana of some unknown, unreal afterlife. There were many aspects to the Lord and, while Casey often had sneered at each and every one of them, there were still times when he had felt a reality to their existence that transcended his own daily life.

At this moment, he felt no desire to sneer.

"Move it, you two," their contact said in a low icy voice that could not have carried much beyond them. "You in the middle, keep walking stately, erect. But you other two, on the sides, I want to see some movement from you."

He was lying face down on his bed and it was hard as a rock. In fact, it felt as if it had rocks in . . . suddenly Skarys snapped to full consciousness. He started to get to his feet. As he did, someone gently grabbed his shoulder. Skarys twisted around to get out of their grip, at the same time swinging out with his arm. The effort sent a stabbing pain flashing through the back of his head and he fell heavily on his other shoulder, rolling over on his back then sitting up quickly as the sharp corner of brick stabbed him in the spine.

A young black man was squatting half a meter away from him, grinning. "You all right?"

"Lord, what did they hit me with?"

"This." The black man held up a piece of brick.

Skarys put his hand to the back of his head, finding the tender spot where he had been hit. His hair was sticky with dried blood but there didn't seem to be any serious damage. It was Poley's turn to do for Skarys what Skarys had done for him the night before, but Poley was nowhere around.

"They told me to take care of you, to keep you safe. I think they wanted me to hit you with this again but not me, no sir. I may be crazy but I ain't stupid."

"How much damage did they do to me?"

"Not much. Just a little cut. I looked at it while you were sleeping. You got something to put on it?"

"Not with me." Skarys got to his feet slowly. The pain had turned to a dull throb that had decided to take up residence in his forehead, although the tender spot on the back of his head still shot out rays of agony whenever he made a quick movement. They had done a good job of keeping him off their trail. He turned to the black man. "You going to try to stop me?"

The man held up one hand in a gesture of defeat, and displayed the stump of his other arm. "Like I said, I ain't stupid."

"Which way did they go?"

He pointed in two directions, hand one way and stump the opposite. "That way."

"You trying to be funny?"

"They split up. They didn't know where Marten was going and I sure as hell don't know either."

Skarys wondered how long he had been out. It was already quite dark. The Lady would be angry with him—he had let her down; he still hadn't paid off his debt.

There was a murmur from the ragpickers in the empty buildings around him, a murmur with an undertone of excitement. He could see them moving out and looking, peering back in the direction of the old warehouse.

There, in the distance, moving toward them, bright lights high in the air, shining down . . . and he knew why they were murmuring, what they were excited about.

He would have to move, move fast, to stay ahead of svana. Even now, youngsters were running eagerly up the street toward The Point, eager to be the first to spread the news.

Skarys moved at as fast a walk as his head would let him. Soon it would die down and he would be able to move faster.

He would find the girl and bring her back to The Lady if it took him all night long.

Red motioned Flyte to stop and they sat down on a crumbling wall. Ahead of them, on a lower level, Kip and the tuft had done the same. "They're stopping too often," he said. "She's slowing him down. Skarys'll catch up with them sure as shit."

"Maybe not. You really knocked the hell out of him with that brick."

Red grinned. "Nah. His head is just as hard as mine." He looked back in the direction they had come. If Skarys was back there, it was too dark to see him. The lights of The Point were in their faces and Skarys would be able to see him and Flyte easier than they would be able to see him, and he could slip right past them, around them, and get to Kip and the tuft while he and Flyte Error were still too far away to do any good. Maybe they ought to catch up with Kip.

Red had another idea. "You keep following them. I'm going to get a little higher." He started for the old rusted fire escape then stopped. "What the hell is that?"

Behind them it was no longer dark with only the fires of the reclamation plant glowing dimly behind the buildings. Now there was something brighter, lights that seemed to be moving toward them although Red couldn't be sure.

Flyte joined him and looked toward the lights. "Hey, you know what, Red? I think it must be svana tonight."

"You might be right." Red whooped then started to run in the opposite direction. "Come on. We got to tell Kip."

Bluebird pulled away from Kip when they reached the street where Kip had first intercepted her. How long ago had it been since that moment? Was it only hours? It seemed like days to her. "I can find my own way home from here," she said. "I don't need your help any more. I know where I am now."

"Look, it's not that I don't like you." He took her chin in his hand and looked earnestly into her eyes.

"You said you wanted nothing to do with me, just because I live with The Lady."

"It's not that."

"It is!"

"I . . . it's all so damned confusing." He looked miserable. Bluebird wanted to console him, to feel his head against her breast, but she wouldn't allow herself to be so weak.

"Goodbye." She turned away from him and started moving swiftly down the street.

He followed and danced around her, to her side, in front of her. "Bluebird. Please. Listen to me. Just listen to me." She pushed him aside.

The streets of The Point were still alive with people and many of them seemed to be amused by this show. Well, let them. Actually, she was probably safer with Kip prancing around her like a lovesick fool than if the two of them were walking side by side, and especially if she were alone. She'd let him talk a little longer, until she got into her own neighborhood, within distance of The Lady's house. It was a small price to pay.

Her own neighborhood. It wasn't her neighborhood; it was The Lady's. She belonged here in The Point, with Kip.

"Go ahead," she said haughtily, not looking directly at him. "Say whatever you have to say."

"Look, I'm sorry about what I said before."

She said nothing.

Kip was now walking along beside here but still gesturing wildly, half-turned toward her. "It's just that. . . well, hell, Bluebird, I'm scared of The Lady. Everyone is."

"There's nothing to be scared of."

"Well . . . maybe not for you."

And she wasn't scared of The Lady. Not any more. She had been cowed by her in the past, for the last year or so, but not any more. She was her own woman now and she would do as she pleased, and The Lady be damned.

"And don't call me Bluebird. That's not my name any more."

"Well, what should I call you then?"

"I don't know yet."

Someone called Kip's name and he turned to see Red and Flyte more than half a block behind them.

"Your friends want you." She turned around and began walking again.

"Let them catch up with us if they want me so much."

Bluebird felt a tiny twinge of panic—part of her was glad that Kip wanted to stay with her; she wondered if she'd ever see him again if they separated. Yet she didn't want to be in the company of his friends. She couldn't fight all of them if they wanted to lead her elsewhere; she wasn't even sure she could keep her composure around all of them.

"Kip! It's svana night."

"What?" They both turned as the Red caught up with them.

So close. They were on the edge of The Point, only a few blocks away from The Lady's home. "How do you know?" she demanded.

"We could see them coming." Red stopped to get his breath. "They're coming from Westmeat. We could see the lights. You can't mistake svana."

"But I thought . . . " Bluebird remembered what Gloria had told her to tell The Lady.

Kip looked at her intently. "You thought what?"

"Nothing."

Red laughed. "The Lady knows all. The Lady sees all. The Lady tells all." Red leaned forward and said harshly into Bluebird's face. "But sometimes The Lady lies!" He leaned back and laughed some more.

"I've got to get back to The Lady."

Red held up his hands. "No problem. Let's get the little

lady back where she belongs. Hey, let's go! Hup, two, three, four. Hup, two, three, four." He started marching down the street and the other three followed helplessly behind him.

No matter how you cut it, it was clear to Demon Pawn that it wasn't going to be easy. Marsh was walking like a zombie, which fit his role perfectly, but Pawn could see that he was basically out of it. They were going to have to move quickly and briskly when the time came and Polansky just wasn't up to it. Pawn wondered if the old man had gotten any sleep at all in the past twenty-four hours. He couldn't hold up under all this; he was just too old.

Casey wasn't in much better shape. The 'killers and other drugs could only do so much. He'd lost a lot of blood and he needed rest and sleep. That he could still even stand up said a lot about him.

So it was up to Pawn to keep them together and somehow to keep them going when the time came. He was in the best shape of them all and he was suffering from lack of sleep. His legs felt like they were made of lead and there was a dull ache behind his eyes, which felt sore. All he wanted to do was close them.

"Be ready," a voice hissed. "It's almost time."

They hadn't even reached The Point yet. Why were they wearing these silly costumes if no one was going to see them? But there was no one to put the question to.

"Casey! Marsh! Did you hear that?"

"Yes."

"Right."

It would all be over soon, one way or another, and then maybe Pawn could get some rest at last.

"Human body heat detected."

On the screen, Walston saw the blurry red image moving toward the Ultimate Warehouse. "What the hell's he doing? He's going in the wrong direction. Is that definitely one of our suspects?"

"Unidentified. Definitely not Marshall Polansky or the man known as Casey George."

"Where the hell was he coming from? Move back. Give me a wider view." A river of red suddenly appeared in one corner of the screen. "What the hell is that?"

"There is a large collection of human beings in that area. It has been forming for the past thirty minutes."

"Why the hell didn't you tell me? What's going on down there?"

"The presence of a large number of portable actinic lights along with the presence of a large number of people in this section of the barraque indicates the formation of a svana parade."

Svana! It had been a long time since Walston had witnessed one in person but the very word still sent shivers of an almost religious fervency through him. He remembered when he was much younger . . . he drove that thought from his mind, although it lingered at the edges of his consciousness.

"Do you wish me to withdraw the Speyes, Mister Secretary?"

"No! Why would you do that?"

"There will soon be a large number of HV fliers in the area, as soon as they become aware of the presence of svana. In fact, one has just left and several are already being readied."

"How the hell did they know so fast?"

"The cameras on the city wall have already detected the presence of the lights."

Walston hesitated. If he moved his Speyes, how could he find out what he wanted to know? Yet the price of leaving them in place was too high—some of them would surely be spotted by the HV cameras. There might even be a collision.

"Remove all the Speyes from the barraque except those over the Ultimate Warehouse. Remove those only if a flier comes into the neighborhood. Inform me if you do so."

"Done. There have been further indications that the floodgate in the basement of the Ultimate Warehouse is being activated."

"What indications?"

"Sound waves similar to the previous ones but more protracted and with varying degrees, as if several valves were being opened separately. There has not been any deflection of river currents however."

The red blob appeared again, moving swiftly from the Ultimate Warehouse and joining another figure near the red river of humanity.

"That wasn't Poley, was it?"

"Negative. I have a tentative identification: a Thomas Watson, also known as Demon Pawn."

"What about the person he joined at the svana parade?"

They had merged into that solid red stream and could not be picked out and followed.

"They were too close to the parade. My sensors were too overloaded for any identification at all."

"Do you have any idea where Poley is?"

"Negative, Mister Secretary. He was last observed returning to the Ultimate Warehouse. No further data is available at this time."

Kip had mixed feelings about the sudden appearance of Red and Flyte. On the one hand, it took the edge of out of the argument he was having with Bluebird. On the other hand though, he wanted to be alone with her. "What happened to Skarys?" he asked.

"He needed some rest so I put him to sleep." Red said it with considerable bluster.

"Sure. And I'm going to be on Children of the Undercity next week."

"I used a brick." Red said with a grin.

"What?" Bluebird stopped to turn around.

"I hit him on the side of the head with a brick. What's wrong with that?" Bluebird turned her back to them and started walking again. "Hey, when you're dealin' with a guy like that, you gotta use everything you got. Right, Kip?"

"Lord, you've really put us in trouble this time, haven't you?"

"Not us, Kip. Just me."

"But we're blood."

"Glad to hear you say it. But this is just between me and Skarys. I want you and Flyte to stay out of it. You'd only get in my way anyhow."

"Sure." Kip wasn't sure whether he meant it or not.

"Anyway, I think we're safe from Skarys for a little while longer. Where the hell you goin', anyway?"

"Lady Madonna's."

It was Red's turn to stop on the street. "And you talk about me gettin' us into trouble. What the hell you goin' there for?"

"She lives there."

"Skarys said something about her. I bet he's in her pay. Everybody works for her but us."

"I don't." Bluebird had stopped to rest on the step of a well-kept old house.

"What you live there for then?"

"I don't work for her. Not any more. I'm my own woman."

Kip thought she said it too strongly, as though if she said it loud enough and often enough, it would be true.

Behind them, a woman's voice was raised in song, a hymn of praise and rapture. As they heard it in the distance, Bluebird got up suddenly, a strange expression on her face.

"I've got to get back to The Lady," she said.

Red grabbed her by the elbow. "I thought you didn't work for her. I thought you were your own woman."

"I am. I am!"

"Then what do you have to go back to her for?"

Kip felt strangely frightened as Bluebird and his friend stared at each other for a moment that seemed to last for nearly a minute, though surely it was much shorter. Red had his usual grin pasted on his face, daring Bluebird to answer him, while the stricken look on her face made Kip want to take her in his arms at the same time that he knew that it would cost him if he did so at this time.

"I don't have to go back to her." She started walking back in the direction they had come. "Kip," she said imperiously, "find me a rooftop."

"Oh, she's giving orders now," Red said.

"Find her a rooftop," Kip said tightly.

"How about this one? Will this do, my lady?" Red bowed deeply then pointed to the top of a nearby building.

"How will we get up there?" The imperiousness was gone from her voice.

"Easy." Red leapt for the old fire escape and pulled it down with a protesting, rusty squeal. He held it to the ground with one foot and bowed again. "After you, my lady."

There might have been a rusty squeal in Westmeat too as the timers that Demon Pawn had set under the Ultimate Warehouse finally clicked off their last few seconds, but there was no time for a squeal to make itself known. As the riverbank gates started opening slowly, the river rushed in, pushing aside tortured metal plates that had rusted thin after a century, slamming up against the middle gate, which held firm. Seeking a way out, the river rushed up against the walls and roof of the tunnel, finding an old escape valve and spurting up with increasing pressure, like water in a Venturi tube, crashing through the floor of the smaller building, breaking through electrical lines and the pneumatic tube that had sent the painkillers from the first floor to the third. Then the waters subsided, content to try to fill up the first floor of the building while electrical sparks hissed and broke against the dry wood of the building's timbers.

The svana parade stopped for a moment and their contact jumped off the float and darted into a nearby building. "Follow me!" Pawn and Casey ran after him but Polansky just stood silent in the svana, waiting for it to move again. Casey grabbed him roughly by the arm. "Marsh! Come on! This is it! You've got to go now!"

Marshall shrugged him off, never looking at Casey. "I've got to stay with The Lord. I belong here."

"Marsh! This is your life we're talking about. We can't stay here."

"This is my life. I have children and grandchildren here. I can't leave now."

"Marsh! You don't know what you're doing!"

"Leave him," their contact said in a low voice from the shadows of the building.

"But . . . "

"Leave him!"

Svana began to move again and Marshall Polansky moved forward in his stiff-legged gait, oblivious to the price of his decision, comfortable in his guise of Death, never looking back or to either side, never seeing the pain in Casey George's eyes.

Kip and Bluebird moved swiftly up the fire escape. Red looked at Flyte. "You comin'?"

Flyte wanted to say no. He wanted to go back to the warehouse and plug himself into the computer but how could he ever explain that to Red? But he had to try. "No. I don't think so."

To his surprise, Red said, "Suit yourself," and started up the ladder. It swung noisily back up as soon as his weight was off it and he was standing on the first landing. Kip and the tuft were already out of sight, perhaps even on the roof already. "You sure you don't want to come with us?"

"I want to go back to the warehouse and see what shape our stuff's in."

"Your stuff, you mean."

"Okay. My stuff."

"We're gonna have to find us a new place to crash. That place is getting too crowded."

"Yeah."

"Meet you at The Oyster later."

Red disappeared up the ladder and Flyte began walking back toward The Point, barely able to keep himself from running until he was out of sight. Already the night had become a symphony of female voices raised in praise to The Lord, The Thousand-Gods-in-One. If the svana parade belonged to the men, if they were the only ones to portray Him, to march His thousand-and-one incarnations through the streets of the barraque, only the women were allowed to praise Him, to sing of His glories, His triumphs, and His sufferings, and Flyte was enveloped in their songs and paeans and soon he could not run any longer through the clogged streets.

The night had erupted into dozens of tiny suns, burning brightly on poles moving rapidly through the streets, while other muscular men jogged their way along, carrying on their shoulders the litters and floats of The Lord, portrayed in His thousand-and-one facets, sitting in padmasana, or sidhasana, standing up a silent and unmoving gesture of benediction, or with His arms outstretched in suffering, His face a vision of agony.

He was portrayed by statues and molded effigies but more often than not by living men who maintained their one pose throughout the svana parade from one end of the barraque to the other.

Flyte stood in awe in the shadows, as he had done for all the years of his life, his mind divided in two, one that sneered at this manifestation of religious superstition while the other remained that of the little boy who wanted to follow them all the way to the end, the little boy whose mother had told him that svana came out of the river and went back into it. It made no difference to the little boy then and it made little difference to Flyte Error now. Even the rational part of his mind marveled at the spectacle and admired the strained muscles of those who carried the floats and poles, and the tired taut muscles of those who could hold a pose for so many hours.

Poley was still hacking away at the wires with his knife when he heard a rumble underneath him and the building shook violently. After a few seconds all was silent then the building creaked and settled, seeming to list to one side. Poley went back to the windowframe. The knife was now practically useless—it seemed to take forever to cut through another wire. Sweat stung his eyes.

Then he heard another sound, a crackling sound. He moved around the room, trying to find its location. It seemed to be coming from the first floor. He ran down the stairwell to the doorway. The sound was louder and there could be no doubt—it was the sound of flames in the lower part of the building.

"Get those damn fliers of yours out of my sky!"

"It's not your sky. It belongs to me." Mont'Illiano was not being very helpful.

"I'm asking as a fellow member of the Council. If you want to help me get the web back, I need to observe the entire svana parade."

"No problem. I'll give you access to all of our cameras."

"I need the detail of our surveillance fliers."

"Look, Walston, you've got your job to do and I've got

mine. The whole city wants to watch svana whenever it happens and that's my job. If it gets in your way, well, that's just tough. You'll have to work around it until svana is over."

"I thought we were on the same side," Walston said bitterly.

"Sometimes we are; sometimes we aren't. Right now, I've got a job to do and I'm going to do it. You can have access to all our cameras and that's that."

Mont'Illiano's image was replaced with that of the svana parade moving slowly across Walston's holostage. He hadn't watched a svana parade in years. Even its image brought up memories and emotions he hadn't experienced for a long time, memories and emotions he had wanted to forget. Now he seemed to have no choice but to watch.

And remember.

Bluebird raced up the old iron stairs to the roof of the building and climbed over the parapet. A stiff breeze blew her hair about and she had to keep brushing it from her face. Even now the sky behind them, in the direction of The Point, was ablaze with white light, and women throughout the barraque were praising their Lord. She had only a few moments before the parade would reach them.

Kip climbed over the parapet and joined her.

"No. Stay back. You shouldn't be here at all."

"Why not? Lots of women just sing in doorways with everyone in the barraque around them."

"There are singers and there are singers." How could she possibly explain to him if he didn't already know? However much she might scoff at The Lady, something deep inside her felt this was sacred, something to be done alone and in solitude. Anyway, it was her gift, her only gift, and it was not meant to be spent lavishly. She almost blushed as she realized that she was now thinking in opposite terms from the way she had talked to

The Lady only a few days earlier. And she wondered what she would think and believe in a few days or even a few hours, when nothing was left of svana but memories.

Red Green joined them on the roof.

"Well, well, well. Let's hear our little canary now."

"My name is not Canary."

"Canary, robin, meadowlark. They're all the same. If you want to hear some real singing, little birdie, come to The Zone. We're going to be performing at Cannibal Soup, you know."

"Kip told me," she said stiffly. She wouldn't tell him that she had already seen them perform several times and that she liked them.

"She was at the Money Marriage the other night," Kip said.

"If you two must stay up here, the least you could do is shut up."

Red held up his hands in mock subservience while a hurt look crossed Kip's face that briefly made her feel guilty. But there was no time to feel that way long. Svana was almost upon them, the lights no longer a glow behind them but a mass of separate lights bobbing through the streets of the barraque and the women's voices raised in praise were closer. She could almost smell the incense. She felt frightened and uncertain: she hadn't exercised her voice in more than twelve hours. If she had been at The Lady's she would have had time to do some warm-up exercises but there was no time for that now.

The first of the platforms appeared down the street, a golden Buddha of a man in padmasana as His bearers moved slowly along, the voices of the women surrounding Him moving closer, another voice raised only a few doors down to greet The Lord as He approached. She warbled softly in her throat, a sound that could not be heard more than a few meters away, and she heard Red Green snicker.

She felt anger rise inside her like a pure white flame and she sang louder, using all the techniques she had learned from The Lady without even thinking about them, remembering her wild and impetuous love for Kip Marten, her anger at Red Green, her fear when she had been deep in the bowels of the warehouse, her uncertainty throughout most of the day, and wove them into a wordless song of love for The Lord, anger at His persecutors, fear of all the ills that beset humanity, and the uncertainty of life itself, losing herself in her greatest gift, and using everything she had ever known in her life without thinking or analyzing, expressing with all the gift of her Lord-given voice and the skills that The Lady had taught her.

Pawn had expected that they would go down and follow the tunnels to some place probably near the wall to make their escape from the barraque but instead their contact led them upwards. "Hurry," he said. "We don't have much time."

"We're going as fast as we can," Pawn said. "Casey's injured."

"I'll make it," Casey said through clenched teeth.

At last they reached the roof of the building. The breeze felt good after the costumed exertion of svana. Below them, The Point was ablaze in the lights of svana and the night was alive with voices singing wordlessly but Pawn had little time to appreciate the scene, even had he been in the mood to do so.

Above them was darkness—even the stars had turned off their light for the svana parade. Then a square of light opened in the sky and Pawn was staring into the interior of a flier. "Get in," their contact said. Pawn scurried in but Casey tripped as he tried to enter and sprawled on the floor of the flier, moaning. Their contact pushed his feet in then closed the door and was disappearing back down the stairway even as the flier took off to join its compatriots in the sky.

Pawn turned back to look at Casey but a woman's voice said, "Don't look." He recognized it as the woman who had spoken to him in the warehouse even though her voice was now undistorted. "I'll take care of your friend."

Pawn looked ahead through the windshield of the flier. "How is he?"

"He's lost a lot of blood and he's in shock. We can take care of him though. He'll be all right."

"Why are we following svana? Shouldn't we be leaving the city?"

"Later. If we were to leave the fliers covering svana, it would be noticeable. We'll have to wait. Everything is going according to plan. You've done well, Demon Pawn, but you will have to find a new name for yourself."

"And Casey too?"

"Both of you."

"What about Marshall? He's still down in the svana parade."

"He can't do us any harm. He knows very little; he can tell security about you and Casey but it won't do them any good. No one will know how to find you."

"Maybe." That wasn't what Pawn had meant but there was nothing he or anyone could do for Marshall now. He had to concentrate on his own future and he wouldn't be able to relax until they had left the barraque and the city far behind them. The night had already cost him more than he cared to think about.

There was nothing that Flyte could do that could help Kip and Red but maybe he could help them with the rig.

Heading back to the warehouse wasn't easy. The streets were jammed with excited people and he felt like some kind of fish swimming upstream—he was heading straight toward one of the arms of the svana parade, a multi-limbed beast that streamed up all the main streets of the barraque.

What would Red do in a situation like this? Flyte leapt for the bottom rung of an ancient fire escape but he couldn't reach it.

"Here, little man, let me help you." One of the few laborers not involved with svana held him up and Flyte raced up the escape to the roof of the building, jumping from one to another until he had run out of space. There was no way he could jump an entire street.

He went back down to street level, fighting his way through the people now jammed against the buildings as the parade itself passed through. All around him, women were singing their praises to the Lord. Undoubtedly some of them hoped they would one day take The Lady Madonna's place as the last to sing. Would tonight be that night?

He went down another alley, leapt for another fire escape until he could reach it, pulling himself up, breathing heavily, stopping to rest until he could get his breath back, across a few buildings.

From this vantage point, he could see the end of the parade several blocks away. He watched, a little bit in awe, slowly getting his breath back, then went slowly down this building's fire escape.

The final gate opened and the river waters rushed into the basement of the Ultimate Warehouse and down through passageways into those of many others in Westmeat, some of them already in the last stages of decay, their structures so weakened that it took only this slight undermining of their foundations to cause them to cave in upon themselves, forming tall piles of rubble.

Bricks and huge chunks of concrete came crashing to the ground as the ragpickers and homeless tried to avoid them. Rusted girders twisted, broke apart, and flipped into the air to fall to the earth like giant daggers. Most of the remaining windows shattered, sending rains of glass to the ground.

The Ultimate Warehouse was made of sterner stuff. The walls trembled, several large chunks of concrete and brick broke loose to punch holes in the flooring, and part of the roof caved in, but the walls stayed secure, the building still stood. It was rooted too deep in the earth to be disturbed by a little water.

Despite the water that gushed out into the streets from broken mains and sewers, fires sprang into being as they had in the building where Poley was trapped. Filthy debris spewed out into the gutters and broken sidewalks of Westmeat. The news fliers left the dying svana parade and headed toward the newer and more exciting item, followed quickly by police and medical fliers, searching for the dying and wounded.

One of the fliers flew out across the phosphorescent river and lit on a wall of the reclamation plant, where a cameraman got out and began covering the scene from across the river. As he did, two of its passengers got down through the hatch in the belly of the machine, well protected from any prying infrared or other detectors, and disappeared down an opening in the roof of the building.

Poley yanked frantically at the wires, frustrated by the slowness of his progress, but they only cut his hands and he had to go back to cutting them one by one with his knife, so nicked and dull it was practically useless. The room was getting warm and the smell of burning wood was in his nostrils.

He couldn't wait any longer—he had to get out now, regardless of the cost. He peeled back a large section of wire and glass from the frame, cutting his hands and arms in the process. He hoped it would be enough. He started through the opening, feet first, feeling shards of glass rip his clothes and abrade his skin, the sharp nubs of wire left in the frame poking him and scratching him cruelly as he forced his body over them, till finally he was past, able to inch his shoulders through the last bit, hearing the crackle of flames grow louder, then hanging by his fingertips for a brief moment before letting go, falling onto the cement lip around the building, letting his body go limp and rolling over into the river's muddy bank.

His ankle hurt but it didn't seem to be broken, only sprained. Behind him, the inside of the first floor was alive with flickering flame, mirroring the glow of the recycling plant on the other side of the river.

Then the second floodgate let go and the river forced its way toward the Ultimate Warehouse. The floor of the smaller building buckled and the building seemed to tilt, folding inwards upon itself, then stopped, while the fire seemed to seize the initiative and grew stronger. The first beam fell in a spray of sparks and ashes and charcoal.

Poley didn't wait any longer. He hobbled toward the fence as fast as he could.

Red Green would never admit to himself, much less to Kip and Flyte, any leanings toward religion. He sneered at The Lord, took His name in vain whenever possible, and had nothing but contempt for those who professed belief. Yet he liked the spectacle of svana as much as any believer and even admired those who could sit in one pose for hours without so much as the twitch of a single muscle, even if he saw no real purpose or use for such a talent. And he certainly wouldn't argue with the men who acted as bearers for the floats and lights. He knew the dock and factory workers would make quick work of him.

But he was completely unprepared for the emotions that welled up inside him when the tuft finally unleashed her voice. He had heard many good singers but there was pain and agony and yearning mixed with triumph and joy and elation in her song, and he remembered his own agony of not having parents when he was a child, the cruelty of children who treated him not merely as an outcast and outsider but as an object of derision. *Red, Red, wet his bed.* He turned away, not wanting Kip to see the tears in his eyes. They had been friends for a long time, blood brothers, but Kip had never known him as anything but the hardened bully who would beat up anyone who dared to cross him. He didn't know the pain that Red's childhood had cost him and Red wasn't going to let Kip see this sudden softness that he himself had forgotten.

And then he heard something else in the tuft's song: the unbridled rawness of the riot in his own performance, transmuted by her voice into a thing of beauty as well as of challenge.

Flyte Error was nearly in Westmeat when he felt the earth tremble underneath him. He grabbed hold of an ancient rusted street sign, wondering if it was an earthquake. The trembling over, he continued his flight toward the warehouse, svana now behind him. He had barely gone a block when he heard an explosion ahead of him. What was going on? He continued onward as he heard more explosions, closer and closer to him. When a geyser burst through the pavement half a block in front of him, he finally realized what had happened and figured that Poley had finally opened the lock.

Despite his fright, he kept moving, eager to reach the device. He had to detour around piles of rubble where several buildings had collapsed in the street. The air was full of smoke and it covered his clothes with ash and entered his nostrils, burning his throat and stinging his eyes. The smoke also carried the smell of the foul waters of the river. Fireplanes appeared in the sky, fighting for space with the HV fliers. He had to stop frequently to wipe the soot from his tear-filled eyes.

Lady Madonna barely had time to do her voice exercises before svana would arrive. She pushed back the knowledge that Bluebird wouldn't be here to show off her voice; she would deal with that issue later. Perhaps one of those voices in the distance was Bird's; she didn't recognize it but it could easily be hidden in all those voices.

Her own voice was no longer the instrument it had been twenty years earlier, when it had silenced all the other voices in svana, when all recognized her preeminence and she had reigned supreme, given the final spot at the end of the svana parade, so all would hear and know there was no singer who could come close to matching her.

Those days were gone but she could still measure up to the best of the current singers. She had reigned longer than any other singer ever had but she reigned no longer, except that no other singer had arisen since who shone so clearly above all others. Until then, all singers would sing as they pleased, and there would still be many singing when the parade finally lost itself and disbanded at the other end of the barraque.

She went out to the front of her house and waited. To climb to her roof or anyone else's was too much of a chore for her now and few would be watching in this section of the barraque anyway.

And then she heard the voice, rising effortlessly over the others, partly because it was so close but also because it was so strong and pure. It took her breath away and for a moment she didn't recognize it. But then there was a familiar turn of phrase and she knew that the voice belonged to Bluebird, somehow stronger, clearer, and more beautiful than it had ever been before.

That was the beauty of svana: it made the adrenaline flow, as in an athlete before a big game, and you either stumbled or you soared. The Lady smiled, knowing that her lessons had taken hold, hearing them in Bluebird's voice, and listening as one by one the other voices trailed off and Bluebird was alone in the svana night. It was as she had hoped: her successor was her own student and all was well.

But she herself had yet to raise her voice on this svana! It had been over thirty years since there had been a svana without her voice.She was tempted, sorely tempted, to sing anyway, but she knew she could no longer match Bluebird and that everyone in the barraque would hear and know. And how could she face

Bird then?

Nonetheless she sang softly to herself as the lights approached and engulfed her, and she was surrounded by silent men and banners, colorful costumes and clothing, the only sound the rapid pounding of feet, the flapping of flags in rapid passage, and Bluebird's songs of praise, still rising over the nearly silent men and the few shouts and cries from the people in her neighborhood.

There was joy and sorrow in Bluebird's voice, more joy and sorrow than she could possibly have experienced in her short life, and The Lady was irritated briefly by some passages that sounded like something that Bluebird has picked up in The Zone until she remembered that she had done something similar in her own youth and it had become a standard of the ever-changing svana song of praise, which was not meant to be something static and unchanging but to come from one's own heart and experience, and it was right for Bird to include it in her song, just as it would be wrong for The Lady to include it in hers.

The end of the svana parade was approaching and Lady Madonna looked up to see the tall black skeletal figure of death approaching, almost as if it were coming for her. Trying to catch up with the others, it stumbled, fell, and was motionless on the ground nearby. She ran to his side but he was quickly surrounded by svana outriders.

"No, Lady," one of them said gently. "He is not for you. He is ours tonight. We will take care of him."

They lifted him gently and reverently, and swiftly carried him away in the vanishing parade.

Flyte Error was not the only one racing through the streets of the Point toward Westmeat. It seemed that all of the barraque, rogues and gentlefolk alike, were rushing to gawk at disaster and bear witness to tragedy. Two spectacles in one night! It was a treat beyond price.

Of course most of them hoped to profit from their trip with something more tangible than memories of crumbled buildings and broken bodies. The squids were barely able to do more than protect the ambulance crews. Souvenirs were easy to come by.

The warehouse was still standing though the way to their entrance was blocked by a pile of still smoldering rubble, but the fence that had protected it was breached in numerous places and ragpickers and other 'quistes trampled nonchalantly over the places where it had fallen. The water came almost halfway up the first flight of stairs.

Doily was standing on the first floor of the warehouse with Kip's autar in hand. He looked at Flyte as he approached and held the autar out. "This yours?"

"It's Kip's. What does the place look like?"

"Not bad. Considering."

Their belongings were still there. Flyte and Doily gathered them together in one room. "Will you guard these for me and Kip and Red?"

"What's in it for me?"

"Well, you and Red, you're blood, aren't you?"

"Not quite."

"You need credit?"

Doily grinned, took out his ear, thumbed it for a few moments, and held it out for Flyte to see. It registered three and a half reaggies.

"If you'll guard these for us while I go check out something, I'll send some credit your way."

"Legit?"

"Sure. We been doing it for a couple of days. It works."

"Okay. Go do your thing. And if I don't get the credit, I'll find another way to get it from you."

Flyte headed for the vault—something that big and heavy would still have to be there. It was at an angle where the floor had buckled underneath it but, when he thumbed the combination, it opened slowly and ponderously as usual. He hit the inside switch. For a moment nothing happened, then he heard a loud hum that ended as the lights came on. He closed the door, leaving it still slightly ajar, still unsure as to whether he would be able to get out if it closed completely and left him trapped there for a slow death.

He plugged himself into the rig. After the usual brief disorientation, he flew toward a Speye. "Find Skarys for me," he ordered.

"Nicholas Skarys?"

"Yes."

"Authorization code, please?"

Flyte dipped into his hidden Benj Walston file, found the code, and reported it to the Speye in milliseconds. The Speye immediately took off, with Flyte along for the vicarious ride. In ten seconds it had identified Skarys's thermoprint. He was about three blocks behind Kip and the tuft, only slightly ahead of the svana parade, running alongside him on parallel streets. Flyte examined the specs for the Speye. It had two lasers. He commandeered another Speye for backup, just in case.

"Destroy the corners of those two buildings." He set up successive crosshairs where he wanted the lasers, and the Speye fired, sending large chunks of concrete crashing into the street, blocking Skarys's path, who stopped and looked up.Could he see the Speye? He then took an alleyway to the next street and Flyte pulled the same trick. This time there was no doubt that Skarys had seen the lasers if not the Speye.

That and the svana parade, now ahead of Skarys and blocking off any access he might have to Kip's location, should do the trick.

Flyte relaxed then he realized what he had done. Skarys would undoubtedly get word to Walston of what had happened and then Walston would have solid evidence that something strange was happening in the city computer and, knowing about the device and its abilities, he would put two and two together.

Flyte ordered the second Speye to crash into the rubble and ordered the other one back to its high-level surveillance then began erasing every trace of what he had done. It wasn't easy—though the computer worked in nanoseconds, Flyte's mind worked only in milliseconds.

The svana parade had barely passed when Skarys called.

"Where are you? Do you have her?" Lady Madonna asked immediately.

"She got away from me."

"Got away?" The problems of this svana night were not over.

Skarys explained what had happened. When he told her about being hit with a brick, she couldn't help but smile slightly.

"Then, as I was about to catch up with them, one of Walston's damn flying Speyes blocked the street so I couldn't get through."

"What are you talking about?"

Skarys told her about the Speye causing the rubble to fall. "If I didn't know better, I'd swear one of those kids caused it. But that's ridiculous."

"Try to find her and bring her back to me."

"I will, my Lady. I've got a score to settle with those guys."

Lady Madonna stood there in the street, the ear still in her hand. Skarys's report puzzled her. What was going on? If there were only some way that she could talk to Walston.

Svana was over. Kip held the exhausted Bluebird in his arms while Red stood at the edge of the roof, looking away from them, apparently doing his best to look as if he hadn't a care in the world.

"That was beautiful," Kip said. "I've never heard anything so beautiful."

"Yeah," Red said. "It was pretty damn good."

"I've got to get back to The Lady," she said. She was exhausted, drained.

Kip helped her to her feet. "Bluebird, I never heard anything like . . . "

"My name's not Bluebird any more." She tried to put some snap into her voice but she didn't have enough energy left. She looked toward Red. "My name's Meadowlark now."

"Okay. Is it all right if I call you Lark?"

She smiled wanly. "Sure."

Another ay-kay. So what? Nearly everybody used them. Maybe some day he'd get tired of being Kip Marten and would take a new name, just like Flyte and Bluebird/Meadowlark and Lady Madonna. Someone had once told Kip that if you knew someone's true name then you knew their soul. Well, in that case, everyone could look into his and he didn't care. And, even though he didn't know Meadowlark's true name, he knew her soul, for she had flung it into the evening air only a few minutes earlier.

She leaned on him as they slowly went down the fire escape and covered the few blocks left to Lady Madonna's house.

Red Green stayed a discrete distance behind them. When they reached Lady Madonna's, he said, "Okay. You got her here. Let's fly."

"No. I'm going to stay with Lark."

Red said something undecipherable under his breath. "I'll be at The Oyster when you want me." And he was gone.

Lady Madonna's door opened before they got there and The Lady's formidable bulk came out to take Meadowlark from Kip.

"No," he said. "I've got her."

Meadowlark just smiled and clung more tightly to him.

Walston could find no sign of them. Svana was over and

the news fliers had departed, leaving the skies free for Walston's spies, but there was no sign of any of the laboratory burglars or of Poley. Westmeat was now a jumble of hastily-rigged lights and hospital and police fliers, forcing Walston to leave that area free of Speyes for the time being.

Walston walked into his living room. He was in no mood for Stefan Coldrider. "Clear the wall," he said, and the wall became transparent. Looking down from the top floor of the Tower, everything became just patterns of light, the distance of the barraque broken by the activity in Westmeat, barely perceptible at this distance.

Benj Walston sighed and sat down, brooding over his domain like a disgruntled Zeus.

Pawn and the woman walked down a sheet metal ramp, their footsteps seeming to reverberate endlessly. It went down at a fairly steep angle until they reached a level concrete corridor. The woman, covered in a shapeless gown, her head and face covered by a shawl and veil, stopped and a doorway opened for them. Stretcher bearers carried Casey in and the door closed behind them.

"What's going to happen to him?" Pawn was lost and frightened now that all control had been taken from him.

"We'll do some emergency work on him then send him to another city where he'll get whatever care he needs."

"Will I see him again?"

"No. You'll be sent to different cities."

"I'll know no one. "I'll have no friends."

Now Pawn was truly frightened. He was beginning to understand how Marshall Polansky had felt. He was leaving his beloved barraque forever, the area he knew as well as any man. He could never learn a new city that well; there were many places a child could go with impunity where a man would be challenged. He would be alone in a city of strangers. Was his involvement worth it, when its price was his identity?

"We will, of course, help you get established."

She showed him to a room with an opulence he had never known: a bed so soft and deep it seemed to sink down almost half a meter under his weight; taps with hot water at one, cool and clean water at the other; a refrigerator full of dainties and beverages such as he had never known. A hot meal was waiting for him, reminding him of how long it had been since he had eaten, so long that his stomach had quit reminding him. A holostage waited his command for any shows in the city; she showed him how to use it, leaving him alone with a view of Westmeat on fire, buildings crumbled into massive towers of rubble.

But he was too tired to watch HV for long and the food did not stay in his stomach. He had trouble sleeping—the bed was far too soft. Falling asleep, he would roll over and then wake up, grasping for something to hold onto. He finally pulled one of the blankets off the bed and rolled up in it on the floor.

He awoke to the aroma of hot food. This time his stomach accepted it without complaint. The HV was still on: it was showing some ancient children's show.

He was nearly through breakfast when the woman's voice said, "Are you ready?"

He looked around but she wasn't in the room. "Ready for what?"

"We need to debrief you. We need to know everything that happened."

"How do I know you're not the squids?"

"Would they have treated you like this?

"Who knows? I guess it doesn't make any difference though. You've got me, whoever you are. Go ahead."

They spent the next few hours questioning him about what had happened to him in the past few days. There were several other questioners besides the woman, the rest of them male, one of them sounding quite old. He never saw them. They particularly wanted to know what had been taken from the lab in addition to the copies of the documents in the director's lab.

But Pawn had never seen what was taken, neither when they had broken into the lab nor when they had dumped everything into the Kandalis Reclaimers refuse bin.

They left him alone for several hours then had another question session but by now it was obvious their hearts weren't in it—he didn't have the information they wanted. Even Casey George might not have it. Only Marshall Polansky could help them.

After another night's sleep, the woman returned and led him to another room and motioned him toward what looked like a large closet.

"What is it?" he asked.

"A transplat."

"I've never been in one. What do I do?"

"Nothing. You just go in and stay still until the door opens."

"Can't we do this some other way?"

"No."

There was no arguing with the flat certain tone of the woman's voice. Pawn walked hesitantly toward the closet, stopped, and looked at the woman before finally entering. The door closed behind him with a finality that was frightening.

"Stay as still as possible," her voice said.

Pawn sat down on a bench in the closet, opposite a green light. A sign lit up briefly: he barely had time to read "Scanning" before it went off and the green light blinked red and then green again almost immediately.A few seconds later, the door opened and a pleasant-looking woman gestured him out to a bright sunny day. He looked out the wide windows to surf breaking several stories below him. He had no idea where he was.

Before he left the vault, Flyte Error transferred credit from the government to Doily's account and a little more to each of theirs. It was easy. After all, it was nothing but moving electrons around, and the government accounts still showed the same amount of money, no activity of any kind. Flyte was amused. He was making money out of nothing.

Poley's entire midsection was wrapped in bandages, covering the cuts and gouges he had received at the riverside building. There were numerous smaller bandages on his legs, chest, and arms, leaving still smaller scratches and bruises uncovered. They were hidden by his clothing but he had showed some of them to Skarys.

"So you let the kid get away, huh?"

Skarys, sitting on the other side of the table in a dark unnamed bar on the Westmeat side of the Point had his own bandage on the back of his head. "You ever try running with a splitting headache?" he growled.

"And you're gonna let him get away with it?"

Skarys grinned then winced. "For a while. Let him worry about me, try to keep out of my way, then just when he gets cocky and thinks he's gotten away with it, when he thinks I've forgotten about it . . . " Skarys ground his muscular hands together. "And you? You gonna let those two do what they did to you?"

Poley was quiet for so long that Skarys thought he had forgotten the question or not even heard it. Then Poley emptied his drink and held the mug over the table. "They can't stay underground forever. They've got to come out sometime. And when they do . . . " He slammed the container to the table.

"Lots of luck," Skarys said.

"You too."

"I don't need it. I've got these." Skarys held out his hands, the fingers curled up like animals poised to strike.

The door to the transplat opened and bright sunlight

flooded into the compartment. A pleasant young woman looked in. "Casey George?"

Casey got up from the bench. He had no idea how many days he had spent in and out of consciousness. There was still some tension and soreness in his body but the worst was long gone.

"Are there any men in this organization?" he asked.

"Oh, we have a few." She helped him out even though he felt he no longer needed any help.

"Where am I?"

"This is one of the wilderness areas."

Trees surrounded the transplat, which was outside a large rustic building. The air felt incredibly sweet and fresh, the kind of air that no 'quiste had ever felt. The faint smell of smoke reminded him of the endless fires of the homeless in the barraque. There were strange twitterings and rustlings in the trees around him.

He looked up to a bowl of blue sky larger and wider than anything anyone had ever experienced in the barraque. It was as welcome as the endless realm he had known in space but somehow the blue made it seem friendlier and less cold and uncaring.

"You will complete your recovery here then join in the work. You will be trained by a man." She smiled.

"And Pawn?"

"Your companion is elsewhere. Your other companion . . ."

"Marshall Polansky."

"I regret to say that he has expired. He was old."

Yes, Casey thought, but he never got to see his grandchildren one more time. He looked around again. Mountains rose behind the trees on one side—a short distance away, a torrent of water tumbled over rocks and boulders a hundred or more feet below them.

"In time, we will be able to let your father know that you are well."

Casey nodded. Both he and The Old Man Himself had known that getting involved with the movement was dangerous, but neither of them had imagined the possibility that Casey would wind up in one of the wilderness areas. There were worse places to be.

It had been a long day for Lady Madonna. First there had been the man who had collapsed practically at her front door. She was certain that the man had been Marshall Polansky and just as certain that he had had a massive coronary. She would find out soon enough; for the moment he was a problem for the svana parade people. Finally there was svana itself with the beauty of Bird's voice and her own disappointment at not having a chance to sing for the first time in over thirty years.

And then Bluebird had returned, with her young man. But she was no longer Bluebird: she had become Meadowlark. And that was appropriate. After her performance that night, she needed a new name to fit the new person she had become. But she was emotionally and physically drained and she was asleep before The Lady and Kip Marten had put her to bed.

Marten himself wasn't as bad as she had feared. Though obviously frightened of Lady Madonna, he had stood his ground until he felt his duty to Bluebird . . . to Meadowlark had been done. Then she had asked him to sit down, trying to make it not sound like an order, but his fear of her was obvious. The teacup she gave him clattered whenever he picked it up and he would quickly put it back down.

"I'm not angry with you, Mr. Marten." Actually, now that Bluebird was safe, she was amused.

"I . . . I don't care really." His weak attempt at bravado was also amusing but she had to contain herself and not let the young man see her feelings. He was not a bad young man but he was no Tor Rosedahl. Very few men were.

"You like Bluebird, don't you?"

He was quiet for a moment, obviously gathering his thought. "I like Meadowlark a great deal."

"Meadowlark. Yes. It will take me a while to get used to calling her that."

The HV came to life, with news of the fires in Westmeat. Kip looked at the scenes with horror.

"I'm afraid I'm going to ask you to leave . . . Kip. It looks as if I am going to have a lot of work to do. And I'm sure you would like to get back to your home. But please come back tomorrow. I'm sure that Blue . . . Meadowlark would be happy to see you."

Marten left and she went to work. There were many debts to call in, too many, as she arranged housing for those who needed some place to sleep, medical help for those who were not hurt badly enough to be taken by the city ambulances, trying to reunite separated friends and families, doing the thousand and one things she had to do to make sure all her people were taken care of. She would collect new debts from this but not enough to make up for those she had had to use.

There were still many things to do but the essential things had been done and she was as weary as Bluebird had been. It had been a long, eventful day.She couldn't remember another like it.

"Mister Secretary Walston would like to speak with you, my lady."

It took a few seconds for the import of the computer's words to reach her. The day of unprecedented, unexpected events was not yet over. She and Walston had been adversaries for more than half her life and it had been years since they had last faced each other directly.

"I'll see him in the parlor." She started toward the room where she received her customers.

Benj Walston was waiting for her, standing in front of a chair on the holostage. She sat down in her own chair and initiated the transmission of her own image to his apartment.

"Good morning, my lady." He bowed slightly.

"Good morning, Mister Secretary. I hope this won't take long. It's been a very long day for me and I'm quite tired."

"I understand. It has been the same for me." The years had taken their toll on him—there were crows' feet around his eyes that hadn't been there twenty years ago and the clear unblemished face was now heavily lined. Like hers, his body had grown thicker around the waist. "It's been a long time since we've talked directly but I need your help."

"I am at your service, Mister Secretary."

"I am trying to locate three barraquistes who were involved in a break-in at the starship laboratory several days ago." Lady Madonna remained quiet. "They are currently known as Casey George, Demon Pawn, and Marshall Polansky."

"I know them."

"Will you help, my lady?"

"Why should I?"

"They took the only prototype for a device that was designed to control the starship. It was developed privately by Daul Magwin, who died recently. We can't replace it easily."

"I must protect my own people, Mister Secretary."

"I promise you, my lady, we will not harm them or try to rehabilitate them in any way. I just want to get that device back."

"There are many rumors that the jobs the starship provided in the barraque are going to be eliminated soon."

"That type of work isn't going to be needed much longer."

"My people need jobs, Mister Secretary."

"I will do my best to see that other types of work be routed to the barraque."

"And I will do my best to find out what I can about the men and the device that you seek. Do you have any photographs or descriptions of it?"

"Computer, send Lady Madonna all the information we have on the pilot communications web."

"She is not authorized to receive it, Mister Secretary."

"I am authorizing her now."

"Yes, Mister Secretary."

Lady Madonna heard the facsimile terminal in her office come to life. "Could you give me a brief description of this device?" she asked.

Walston sighed. "It was to be used to help navigate the starship, with up to eight people able to experience the computer directly."

Lady Madonna thought of Skarys's account of the Speye's destruction of a building. "Could they control it directly as well?"

"That was its purpose, to control the starship in flight."

Could it be that one of those . . . those children had somehow gained possession of it and was using it? It didn't seem likely but Bird's relationship with this Kip Marten gave her a door to find out.

It would put Walston very much in her debt and maybe some other people as well.

"Let me know as soon as you find anything."

"I will, Mister Secretary."

"Thank you. Good night, my lady."

For a long moment, they stared at each other across kilometers of light pipe then his image disappeared from her stage and he never heard her say softly, "Good night, my love."